DAMNED TO HELL

MIKE SALT

ABOMINATION MEDIA

This is a work of fiction. The characters, incidents, and dialogues are product of the author's imagination and are not to be constructed as real. Any resemblance to actual persons, living or dead, is entirely coincidental. Names have been used with permission.

ISBN: 9781073526109

For Brianna, thank you for always letting me slip out of bed in the middle of the night to write for a couple hours.

For Justin, Kyla, and Lennox... I don't think I could have written this if I wasn't already a Father.

DAMNED
TO
HELL

CHAPTER ONE

That's the moment it changed for me. When I knew I needed to be here and find help," the fat man said as tears rolled down his chubby cheeks and down his thick neck. The fat man tried to smile, but it fooled nobody. He nodded his head as he tried to keep his composure. The man held strong for a moment before his lip began to quiver and the floodgates opened. He threw his hands to his eyes and began to sob, longer than Rob thought a man should cry in public.

Rob tried his hardest to care. He wanted to feel for the man that was in the same place he had been only a couple years ago. Rob put himself in the fat man's shoes and tried. Ultimately, it meant nothing. The fat man shouldn't be crying like this.

Every Tuesday and Thursday, with the third Saturday of each month, this was where he'd be. The people were always the same. They were either the ones that have lost all hope or just giving it a shot. Rob looked around the small room. Besides the fat man, there weren't a lot of new faces. The same people were here week after week, barely making it day-to-day. With a slight gust of wind, they would snap like a fragile thread holding onto a button threatening to pop off. He was reluctant to come at first, spending the majority of his time drunk or working on getting drunk. Rob started by drinking a six-pack after work, passing out as soon as 8 o'clock rolled around. Then that six-pack turned into two. Not enough time in the afternoon to drink? Rob decided that a couple of beers before work wouldn't be the worst idea. Soon he was drinking on his lunch break. He had on more than one occasion woke up on his front lawn after passing out before he got through the door. It didn't take long for his wife to file for divorce.

That was the worst thing that could have happened to Rob. He began to blame her on quitting. Blaming her for everything bad that happened around them. He wished that she understood the pain he was in because if she was, she didn't act like it. One day she packed her bags and moved out. He didn't speak to her for another three years.

Eventually, she began calling him on Christmas.

About six months ago she gave her yearly Christmas call. She seemed happy. Her voice was the saving grace that Rob needed to hear. That call saved his life. She told him that she had met someone and that they were getting married the following week. That night he hung up the phone after only a short conversation and decided that he wasn't going to quit just yet. He needed to change his life around. The next day was a Tuesday, his first meeting.

"Thank you, Peter," Marla said. The fat man gave a faint smile and sat back down in his folding chair. Marla looked around for someone else to share their story.

An opportunity to talk about how much of a waste their existence had become. A chance to rattle on about things that everyone in the room could relate too, but everyone talked as if they were the only ones with this problem.

Rob often wondered what similar support groups talked about? Was it as self-serving? Did the people there leave feeling like something in this was getting better? That maybe it was all worth it in the end? Rob never felt better after leaving a meeting. Maybe he didn't put his heart into it like he hoped he would. Maybe he wasn't ready for the meetings.

The smell of burned coffee and the coldness of the room was the only thing Rob actually liked about these meetings. The meetings didn't give him a safe feeling; actually, it did quite the opposite. He felt like he was in a dark cave, hidden from society. No better than the bat shit that formed at the floor. He didn't deserve to be happy, not yet. Rob had to earn it. He needed to stick it out and come out the other side a better, stronger man. That's what he thought, nothing yet had proven him otherwise.

The fluorescent lights of the Living in Faith Church gave off a yellow light glow to the room. The church was old enough that Rob remembered his mother dragging him to the bathroom and swatting his bottom when he wasn't behaving well enough in front of God. That may have been over 30 years ago, but the church still looked the same. The walls used to be white, but have dulled with age and look like a chain-smoker took up residence in the small room. Framed pictures of lighthouses and bright sunny skies hung randomly on each wall, the dust on the frame thick enough it could be seen from where Rob sat. The small group of eight sat in a semi-circle in foldable metal chairs. In front of them was the head of the church, long gold curtains hang from the ceiling to the floor, pulled back they would reveal a mediocre painting of Jesus walking with small children, tonight the curtains were closed.

Marla swept her blonde hair from her shoulder, smiling around the room and looked at Rob. Her smile folded inward for a moment before she perked back up and she moved on to the next person, "Jenny?" She said with a nod.

Rob rolled his eyes and slouched as deep into his metal chair as he possibly could, swirled the remaining black coffee around in his small Styrofoam cup and sipped like a grade school kid slurping soup from a spoon.

A petite red-head in an obnoxious blue sweater stood up, "Hello everyone."

The group greeted her, including Rob.

"Today was hard," Jenny began in a whisper. "I know that it's hard for everyone. I know that I shouldn't dwell on it, but..." She trailed off as her whispers cracked and her voice bounced in pitch. "... but next month will be another anniversary."

Rob rolled his eyes far into the back of his skull.

Shit, this again?

Rob stood up and moved to the long table to the side of the room, he pulled the coffee pot out and topped off his small cup. He reached into his pocket and pulled out his phone, opened to the home screen and distracted himself on a social media feed. After a moment he looked up and accidentally locked eyes with Marla, she raised her eyebrows and her eyes grew wide. Her thin face was pulled tight and her lips mouthed the word *sit.*

With the phone back in his pocket, he flopped back into the chair, placing his cup of coffee on his knee. His giant body size made the chair look like a child's chair.

8 o'clock couldn't have come sooner as Rob picked up his chair, folded it, and placed it with the other chairs. Most of the regulars grouped together and chatted about how proud they were of one another, and how much progress they've made.

No one approached Rob.

They used to, but Rob made sure to shut that down right away. He wasn't here to make friends. He didn't care to hear Jenny or Peter's story. They were all the same. My life is a mess. I'm a mess. I hate myself for this. I hate myself for that. Same stories every time.

Rob didn't care about anything but seeing this through. He told himself after every meeting he was getting closer to beginning a new life again.

"Don't forget that Thursday's meeting is canceled, but next Tuesday we will meet again! Saturday's meeting has been moved to 10PM! Don't forget!" Marla said to the few of those left.

She watched as the room emptied and eventually the only person left in the room with her was Rob. He poured more coffee in his disposable cup and stirred it with a straw. She had seen him do this before, many times in fact, though she could never recall him ever pouring any creamer or sugar into the cup.

Marla supposed whatever he was stirring hid in a flask in his jacket pocket.

Figures, she thought to herself, he wouldn't be the first person to do so here.

She didn't blame him. She would need alcohol too if she was in his shoes. Marla folded the last chair and placed it against the wall; she heard the front door open and watched Rob wave goodbye over his shoulder without turning around.

Thank god, she thought to herself. Marla didn't trust Rob, and she hated herself for admitting that. Rob had done nothing for her to feel this way, but it didn't change the fact that there was something about him that scared her. He never truly smiled, he rolled his eyes as people cried or poured their souls in front of strangers. He wore the same navy colored pea-coat every meeting, his face was never shaved and his thinning hair was rarely combed. Rob was never aggressive, as far as Marla could tell, but she wouldn't put it past him that he had gotten into a couple of bar fights when he was younger. Maybe even pushed his wife around a little, which would probably explain her leaving him.

Her heart dropped, *Stop being an asshole, you know nothing about Rob.* Marla would beat herself up for the rest of the night for thinking such a horrible thing about someone she believes needs help.

She poured the remaining coffee down the sink in the bathroom and left it on the counter. Marla turned off all the lights and locked the door behind her as she left.

The cold air pulled the heat from her body as she walked out towards the bulletin board. It was a reminder for anyone that missed her announcement as they left. It read:

"Thurs meeting canceled- -
Will resume next TUESDAY, regular time!!!
SATURDAY meeting moved to 10P!

-GRIEF AND RECOVERY FAMILY SUPPORT GROUP”

CHAPTER TWO

8 o'clock, time to move along to his favorite part of the evening… the local watering hole.

Rob made good time as he sauntered through the park that was the lone obstacle between Loggers Tavern and his support group. He made the same trip after every meeting; he would leave his car in the church parking lot and walk from the tavern back to his car once the night had come to a stop. It started off as an excuse so he could sober up before he got back to his car, but now he actually enjoyed the walk… he looked forward to it. The tall trees and water fountains made him calm down. Rob felt nothing while he strolled under the moonlit path. The path curved and bent obnoxiously as if a drunk that wanted a challenge before he arrived at the bar designed it. A simple thing like a squiggly path would have annoyed Rob generally, but not this trail. Something about it was soothing. He couldn't place his finger on it, but it was what he looked forward to most these nights. He would never admit that, but it was the truth. This was the only time of the night he didn't have the overwhelming desire to drink.

Finally, Rob popped out of the cover of trees and the stone-work fence that bordered Linkville Park. He looked both ways before embracing a slight jog as he crossed the 3-lane road of Bugbear Way.

Rob arrived at the entrance of Loggers. Four dirty brick walls that at one time had been painted white. The outside was littered with spray-paint and sharpie markers. Half-assed attempts of local wanna-be gangstas graffiti. The owner used to have it covered as soon as it appeared, but all that did was give the artists a fresh white canvas. It never stayed white long, and overall it was just a bad idea.

The inside of the tavern fully represented the outside. Cleaning hadn't been a high priority for at least a decade and it looked like how Robert felt. The visibility was limited, half of the light bulbs were dead and appeared to be too much of a hassle to be replaced. The music came from a jukebox that had seen better days and only played hair metal. Two of the three pool tables had books under the legs to level it (although they were still not level) and the dart board had no darts.

Simply put, the bar was horrid. The loyal customers were not there for the music, pool, or darts, they were there for alcohol and not seeing anyone they knew.

They were equally damaged as Rob.

Rob walked up to the bar and nodded to the waitress, Carol.

Carol had worked the bar for most of her adult life. She shared the occasional drink with the customers, sometimes more than the *occasional drink.* She didn't worry about getting dolled up every night, she was content waking up with a hangover and caking on makeup over the previous nights' makeup. Carol was in her late 40s, but the smoke that lingered in the air had sucked another 10 years from her aging skin. She looked like she belonged on the opposite side of the bar, and if she wasn't working at Loggers Tavern, she no doubt would have been a regular.

"How's the night treating you, Rob?" Carol asked as she moved in his direction.

"Nothing a glass of the cheap stuff couldn't fix," Rob said with a smile.

Carol turned around and grabbed from the bottom of the shelf, a dark bottle that boring label read WHISKEY. She poured a couple fingers worth and placed it with a napkin with Rob. Carol propped her hand out, Rob handed her a pre-loaded debit card.

She smiled and turned around to place the card with the rest of the tabs.

Rob often wondered about this lady.

What was her story? She did a good job of faking the smile and playing the game. Carol was here every night, without fail. She never complained. Gave no one attitude. She was liked by every regular, most of which had poured their entire life to her at one point or another. But not one patron could say the same. Even the nights Rob had stayed passed closing hours and split a bottle with Carol, she never told him why she was so broken. Why she had spent the best years of her life hiding in a dark, filthy room that smelled like piss and smoke.

Whatever the story was, Rob would listen. Not "listen" as he did earlier in the night, but actually let the words sink in. When the night came, and it will, that Carol had a little too much of the cheap whiskey and started to form sentences forced through tears.

Sentences that explained the series of events that led her life down the unfortunate path she had found herself down. When the sentences were capped with questions like "why did this happen to me?" and "why did I deserve this?", Rob would be there to help her find the answers.

There would be none to find though.

Rob was still waiting around for those questions to be answered for himself.

"Anything lately from Lanai?" Carol asked as she leaned forward on the bar.

Bringing the glass to his face, gulping down as much whiskey as he could before he answered: "Not as much as I'd like."

"That sucks, hun. I'm sure she'll see how good you've been doing and come around."

"I'm not so sure," Rob said with a slow shake of his head, staring hard at the glass in front of him. "They got married, d'ya know? Hitched over in Reno."

Carol tipped an opened bottle over Rob's glass. "I know, doll, you've told me," she said with a sly smile.

"Oh, fuck!" Rob threw his hands to his forehead, "Am I that pathetic?"

Carol looked around the bar, "Really?"

"Point taken," Rob said as he took a small sip. "Still, doesn't seem like Lan."

"Maybe. I don't know her, so I really couldn't say. And if she is half as pretty as you claim she is, I'm surprised she waited 2 years to remarry."

"Is that supposed to make me feel better?" Rob said with a smile.

"Did you come here to get better?" Carol laughed, "People don't come here to get better, hun. People come here to get worse. To get fucked up enough to forget about today and part of tomorrow."

"How many more of these would it take to forget all of tomorrow?" Rob held the glass out in front of him.

"How much money do you have?"

Both of them laughed.

"Ma'am?" Rob heard a pug looking man at the far end of the bar ask for Carol, he held a dollar bill in one hand.

"One moment," she said with a wink before turning back to Rob. "Rob, let's move on tonight. Find someone to take home. Just think about it?"

No answer was needed, Rob raised his glass and finished it before rolling his body in the stool looking around the bar.

"Fuck," Rob said as his eyes locked with another man across the bar.

The man was named Eric, a tall ginger that seemed to be perpetually wearing jogging clothes. This particular evening, he was rocking a spectacular matching short-shorts and sleeveless shirt (an American flag frozen mid-wave on the front of his chest). Eric didn't fit the theme of the bar, his joyful demeanor and willingness to engage in conversation counteracted the average patron who just went there to forget they were alive and soak their blood with low quality alcohol. Rob used to see him jog by his house back when he was still married to Lanai. He hated him from the moment he saw him breezing by wearing short yellow shorts with his shirt tucked into the waistband.

If Rob hated him then, he loathed him now.

"Hey, Robbie!" Eric pranced up to him.

"Not tonight, Eric."

"Whoa, someone is having a crumby night?"

Rob rolled his eyes and adjusted his seat away from Eric.

"So, what's new, buddy?" Eric followed.

"Eric, go away. I beg you."

"Everything alright?" Eric plopped down beside him.

Rob let out a moan, "Why are you here?"

"You look like you could use company!"

"I'm here almost every night, you are too. When have I ever had company?"

Eric thought about the question, "I wouldn't know, you don't like to talk."

Rob nodded his head as if that was enough of an answer. He pushed the glass to his mouth and swallowed the whiskey.

"I'm about to take off, how about the next one is on me?" Eric offered.

"What do you want in return?"

"Just keep me company until I take off."

Rob thought about the idea for a moment before waving his hand, "I'm good."

Eric smiled, smaller than usual, and patted Rob on the back, "have a good night, buddy."

Rob pushed his hand into his pocket and retrieved a half-crumbled box of reds and a white bic. Folding open the box, Rob placed a stick between his lips and flicked the lighter to life. Jumping to life the flame danced in the air as he brought it closer to the cigarette. The flame licked the paper and dried tobacco. It gave off a smell that was both chemically and stale. Rob pulled a deep stream of smoke into his lungs and exhaled.

He wasn't always a smoker, it was only officially picked up 5 years ago, but he now smoked every day. Lanai wouldn't allow it, so for the final 2 years of his marriage, he hid it. Not well, but well enough that she didn't bother bringing it up more than a handful of times. She was suspicious at most. Once she was out of his life, it became part of him as much as the scar on his upper thigh. Permanent and ugly.

Rob inhaled and watched the small stick shrink as the flame ate it alive. He thought about the first cigarette he had had when he was a young boy. Dillon Cranston from down the road had peddled his new Mongoose bike down the dirt-road that bordered the ditch that Rob and his childhood friends played in as kids. He sold him and his friends a stick each for $5. They each bought one and threw up after only a couple puffs.

His father smelt the smoke before he could even open the door. Rob hadn't received such a bad beating before in his life. After that moment, he decided that day he would never smoke again.

Young-Rob would be so disappointed as Older-Rob placed a second stick in his mouth and lit it.

CHAPTER THREE

Rob pushed open the door of his single bedroom apartment and folded as he entered. He pushed his body up against the nearest wall and bit by bit stood again. After a couple deep, concentrating breaths he managed to move again, albeit a little lopsided.

He pushed the door shut and fumbled with the locks until he was positive it was done. Rob turned and sidestepped his way into his main room, aiming for the couch, missing and flinging his body to the ground in front of it. The ground rumbled with the thunder of his huge body.

4 hours later he awoke to his phone having a meltdown, the alarm had been going off for a straight ten minutes and it finally completed its goal of waking him up. He rolled over and pressed his palms to his temples, the pressure was good. Rob's head felt like a million beating drums all going off in a pissed off rhythm.

Rob crawled to a knee and plopped his body to the couch, his couch cried for mercy as his weight pushed every spring to its max compression. He reached his hand in between two of the cushions, retrieving his prize. The remote to his TV.

With the sports news reeling off in front of him, he managed to turn the clock off on his phone. Rob reached to the coffee table and grabbed his half done grape sports drink, popped the lid off a bottle of aspirin, he threw the bottle into his mouth and whatever remaining pills landed deep in the back of his throat, he washed it down with the sports drink.

Rob relaxed for a moment, watching his team lose another blow out game. Not surprised. Nothing seemed to go his way in the last 5 years.

Finally, Rob moved to the bathroom and brushed his teeth. He rubbed his face; the stubble was beginning to make him look homeless. His hair was long and unwashed. Over the last few years his hair began getting thinner to the point where his scalp was visible no matter how he combed his hair. It was a dark brown, but the dirt and sweat had made it seem darker than it truly was. Rob spit into the sink and rinsed. Rubbing his face one more time before he left the mirror and switched off the light as he exited.

Rob grabbed his only clean work uniform, gave it a single smell check just in case. It would work for today. Throwing it over his body, he went to the closet and found his work pants crumbled at the floor. The work issued polo was a dark navy, the little red "Tylers Friendly Pump" logo stitched into his left peck, his slacks were a khaki, but the grime had accumulated after the weeks he neglected washing it.

Walking through his small kitchen (that was attached to his main room), he grabbed a banana and headed for the door. Work started an hour ago.

The annoying work-lead screamed his worst insults at Rob, it wasn't anything he hadn't already heard the little 20-something ginger yell his way before. Being late wasn't uncommon, and the fact he showed up at all anymore was surprising to everyone. The angry little ginger finished up his rant and Rob left the center kiosk of "Tylers Friendly Pump", he grabbed a bright reflective vest from a hanger as he exited and went to work.

There was nothing exciting about being a fuel attendant. 48 of the 50 states didn't have them, but Rob found himself lucky enough to live in Oregon where the state demanded it. It wasn't a demanding job and required little to no motivation to excel. Rob walked to the nearest vehicle, which asked for a "fill". Rob grabbed the fuel hose, placed it in the vehicle's gas tank and pressed the necessary buttons that began the operation.

"Aren't you gonna ask for my rewards card?" The young man asked from the car, his hand hung out the car and he held his rewards card out loosely.

Rob rolled his eyes and pushed his palm against the "hold" button with more force than it needed. Grabbing the card from the man, he slid it into the machine which accepted the card with no problem. Rob handed the card back to the man and resumed pumping.

"I appreciate it," the man said as he turned back to whoever was sitting in the passenger seat of his vehicle. Rob overheard him talk under his breath, something to the effect of "these assholes are lucky to have this job and they can barely do it?"

Rob said nothing, he turned around and flipped his finger under the fuel hose, stopping it from pumping any more fuel. It sat lifeless in the gas tank, he walked off and helped the next customer. Sure, he would have to come back and start it again, but the man would have to wait until he had finished a couple customers first. He smiled at the idea of the man getting annoyed behind his wheel, too passive to actually confront Rob.

"Rough mornin'?" Becca asked as she passed Rob. She stood only 4 foot 11 inches off the ground and looked like a small child as Rob's giant 6' 5'' frame walked past her.

"What gave you that idea?"

"Oh, nothing in particular," she said with a smile as she flipped the man's fuel hose back on.

"Wow, I didn't notice, thanks for lookin' out, Becca," Rob said trying to push back a grin.

"I'm sure you didn't," she smiled again and caught up with her giant friend. "So, where'd you wake up this morning?"

"My place."

"Yeah?"

"Yeah."

"Oh, come on. Don't act like it was your bed?" She smiled as she grabbed a debit card from the next customer.

"I did actually."

"Really?" She didn't believe him. "I woke up in my bed, but I didn't drink last night."

"You don't drink," Rob said as he slid the gas hose into a vehicle.

Becca smiled at him, "And you don't wake up in your bed."

Rob hated his job. The summer months were long and hot, he'd sweat off most of the nights' alcohol before noon. Everyone in the city seemed to need gas as they rolled out of town to a lake or to the neighbor towns for shopping. Kids barely old enough to drive rolled in with their Fathers cars and their Mothers debit cards. They mocked and laughed at the mid-30's man as they thought it was never going to be them someday. For most of those little assholes, probably not, but Rob could see their future better than they could. A few of them had the glow of a promising future. College. Careers. Families. Money. Happiness. Others, others didn't have it as nice. They didn't shine as bright; they would burn out with their teen years being the best of their useless lives. These sad souls would most likely end up where Rob found himself. In a dead-end job, and a dead-end life to match.

Before his life crumbled around him, Rob was very pleased with himself and the life he had built around him. A loving wife. A handsome son. A brilliant career.

Brilliant, was a stretch, but he enjoyed it the same.

8 to 5, Monday-Friday with holidays off. Rob would be in his office, tucked behind a computer and a disaster of a desk. He loved his workspace, it was a mess to the untrained eye, but every corner served a purpose. Each pile of papers was stacked with purpose. Each pen and sticky-note left with a reason behind it.

After graduating college from Linkville Art School with a degree in graphic design and web-design, Rob joined a small company and soon moved up the ladder and ran the marketing department. His office overlooked a team of young artists that marketed everything from local car dealerships to nationwide brands like "Apes Brain Dead Thread" a clothing company that was closing in on its record best year thanks to Rob and his team.

Rob could be creative, think outside the box, and make a ludicrous amount of money in the meantime. His 3 favorite things.

He drove a late 60s Mustang, cherry red, and would park it in his own parking spot in the small parking lot behind the building.

Rob loved those days.

He thought about them regularly.

"You with me, Robby?" Becca said as she walked to the next car, "You seemed somewhere else?"

Rob turned to the next car, "What do you need?"

CHAPTER FOUR

Work was long and boring, but it finally ended. Rob clocked out and passed Becca on his way to his car.

"Any plans tonight?" She said as she also clocked out and moved her little feet to catch up.

Rob rolled his eyes, tucked his hair away from his face, "Same as every night."

"So, let me guess?" Becca said.

"No."

Becca pouted her lips, "Why?"

"Because I still have an unbelievable headache and I really don't want to deal with this shit."

"Well, come out with me and the girls?" Becca said as they both arrived at their side-by-side cars.

"Pass."

"Why?"

"I don't have the patience to hang out with 20-something year old girls," he opened his door.

"But we are celebrating!" Becca yelled her last ditch effort.

"Celebrating what?"

Becca rolled her shoulders and gave her best attempt at casual, "Me?"

Rob didn't respond, he just looked at the girl, 10 years younger than himself at least, possibly more. Her short frame had a cute quality to it though. Becca's dark brown hair had natural highlights that most girls paid good money to fake. Her makeup was not overdone, it was just subtle enough to enhance her features.

"I'm graduating tomorrow, you asshole!" She said with a hint of hurt in her voice.

"High School?" Rob said honestly.

"From Tech, Robert! I'm done with this shit finally," she threw her arms out dramatically, displaying the fuel station. "I have an interview Monday, and after I get hired there, I'm gone."

“Congrats, kid,” Rob said. “Seriously, I’m proud of you.”

“Then come out with us! Please, it might be one of the last times we have to hang out.”

“I can’t.”

“What? Are you going to have more fun drinking by yourself in your shitty apartment? Come on.”

“Not by myself,” he said with a small smirk.

“Do you have a date tonight?” Her eyes were wide, part jealous/part surprised.

Rob gave a small laugh and closed the door as he climbed into his car.

He revved up his engine, his late 60s Mustang came to life.

Rob wasn’t lying to Becca, he did have a date. It just wasn’t anything he wanted to share with her. There was no other girl. No dinner. No romance.

Today was the 5-year anniversary of his son’s death, July 13th.

Each year was more difficult than the last. He was told that the only thing that would help would be time, which ended up being a load of shit. It might work for most people, but all it did was give Rob time to get more and more upset. He spent half of his time being depressed, the other half pissed off. There was no time for anything else. If he wasn't sitting in a dark and gloomy bar, he was outside it trying to fight someone.

His son would have been 20. Graduated high school already, working on his second year of college. Jed was brilliant. Handsome. Loved by everyone. His funeral had hundreds of kids showing up, the entire damn school showed up to pay their respect. These were the things that made Rob depressed. His son had so much to offer, so much love around him. There was something about Jed that made people their best. Jed somehow managed to bring the best out of each and every person he was around, including Rob. He had a hard time remembering the last thing he said to his son, and that ate him alive. He wished it was something important. An "I love you" or an "I'm proud of you". Most likely, it was along the lines of: "Don't forget to do your chores when you get home".

He missed Jed. Every fucking day.

Rob poured a glass full of whiskey into a tumbler, sat down in his chair and reached for his phone.

With the glass in his hand, he thumbed through his gallery as he brought the glass to his lips.

Hundreds of pictures in small thumbnails covered the screen, Rob tapped one.

Jed, with the biggest smile on his face, stood beside his father, holding a large Salmon in both hands. They had gone to Clover Cove at the end of June, Jed had pulled in a monster of a fish. It was a proud moment for Rob, his son never gave up. The fish fought him the entire way, and at the end of the day, after the picture was snapped, he shared a beer with his son. As far as he knew, it was his son's first and last beer. A cold one to finish off the day. It was a slow day on the river, but that fish alone made it worth the trip.

Rob scrolled to the next photo, another sip from his glass followed. Jed posed after his last home football game. His bright blue jersey was filthy with sweat and mud. Jed's hair was matted down, the shape of the helmet still formed into his head. Under his arm, the game ball. His coach had given it to him after he sacked the opposing quarterback, forcing a fumble and sealing the win. Sealing a playoff berth for the first time in almost ten years. They lost the first game in the playoffs, but Rob was positive that next year the team would make it even further.

Next photo, Jed sitting at the couch. Nothing particularly special about this photo. Jed looked up at the camera, a half smirk on his face. Rob didn't remember taking the photo, but he looked at the photo the most. Out of the Christmas photos, images of him growing up in different Halloween costumes, the pictures of his first YMCA basketball game, the hundreds of photos of Jed being larger than life... this was the photo he always came back to. It was the last photo his son was ever in. A week before he died. Rob took two fingers and pressed on the screen around his face, the image expanded and surrounded Jed. The smirk. The half-smile he gave on rare occasions. It was the last photo of Jed.

Rob backed out of his gallery, threw the alcohol down his throat and poured more into the glass. His thumb hovered over the screen of his phone for a moment as he thought of his next move. He pressed his thumb on the contacts and scrolled down until he saw Lanai's number, hesitating again he took a long sip from his glass and pressed dial.

The phone rang.

Rob tried to calm his breathing; his heart pounded like the little drummer boy.

"Hello?" Lanai said.

"Hey."

Lanai paused; the silence was horrible. This was a game that was played every year, about the same time of the night. Rob knew how it would play out. He knew it, but he played anyway.

"So, today has been pretty rough," Rob said.

"Yep."

More silence. As each year progressed, the phone call was becoming more and more uncomfortable. Lanai hated July 13th as much as Rob, but she didn't let it control her life. She always took the day off of work, visited his grave, talked to him. Lanai told her son everything that had happened since her last visit (which was a monthly thing). Telling him how work was going, the latest news on Jeds' friends, what she has been up to, but never about his dad. Rob was never spoken of.

"Listen, I can't do this tonight," Lanai said. "I'm sorry."

"I know," Rob bit his bottom lip as his eyes welled up, a tear broke free, running down his face like a hiker running from a mountain lion. "You don't have to be sorry. I just needed to hear your voice."

"Rob, you take care of yourself. Please."

Rob pushed the back of his hand across his face, "No, of course. You too, Lanai."

Click as the phone call ended.

CHAPTER FIVE

Night covered everything in sight. The moon did a poor job of illuminating the world, clouds covered the night sky and hid the stars from the world. The wind blew a silent, gentle breeze through the air, the smell of pine and sap floated through the air.

Rob stumbled from his car; he had given up on the glass of whiskey shortly after the phone call with Lanai ended. The glass only slowed him down. Rob finished the bottle and tossed it somewhere out of sight.

Linkville Cemetery was surrounded by an 8-foot fence. The black bars shot straight into the air, ending in a nice hooked point at the top, a good way to turn away any of the youth who wanted to play "Ghost Hunters" in the middle of the night.

Rob let his left-hand run loosely against the steel bars which made a lovely ding sound as his wedding ring pinged off every other bar. Finally, Rob arrived at the pine tree at the corner of the lot. The lowest branch was thick, it sat only a foot below the fences highest point. At 6 foot 5, the jump was easy for Rob, when he was sober. With a bottle of whiskey in his belly, the jump took numerous attempts and even more f-bombs.

His large hands gripped around the thick branch. Rob took a deep breath and pulled his body up, kicking his legs off the trunk of the tree as he scooted his large body onto the branch. He sat on his butt and caught his breath.

The night was nearly silent, except for the occasional car passing by. A couple houses surrounded the perimeter, but their lights were off and their occupants dead asleep. Not much moved at 3 o'clock in the morning on a weekday.

Rob braced his body on the hook of the fence and slid down the other side. He plopped to the ground, tucking and rolling as he landed.

Drunkenly, Rob had made this walk too many times. It used to be a weekly event, as of recent it only occurred when Rob was at his lowest or on this particular day of the year. He walked up to his sons' tombstone, placed in the far right of the cemetery grounds. The plot to each side of him was vacant, one for Rob, one for Lanai.

Reaching into his jacket pocket, Rob pulled out the crumpled box of reds. He plied out the lone stick and placed it between his lips. The white lighter lit with a single flick, kissing the cigarette and catching it with no effort. The wind was quiet, the smoke floated around his body as he exhaled the plume.

He reached the destination, pausing his body and waiting for his brain to kick his body into auto-drive. Rob never knew what to say when he was here. Did he talk to the tombstone? Did he talk to the ground where his son was buried 6 feet deep? Rob walked up to the tombstone and gave it a pat, like an old friend that he was happy to see.

"Hey, Jeddy."

His voice cracked; the moment caught him off guard. Rob took a moment to regain his composure.

"Hey, Jed," his voice was strong this time, albeit with a slight slurred. "Sorry, it's been so long."

"Meant to come early, but obviously I didn't make it," Rob paused as if he was waiting for his son to reply. "Hope you know I've been doing better. I like to think you already know that. That you are watching down on your Mom and me, checking in on us. I have been attending the classes, haven't missed one. I, um, slowed down on the drinking." Rob held his thumb and pointer finger out in front of him, gesturing the amount he had been drinking. Implying a little, feeling guilty for the lie. "I saw Ms. Thurman the other day. She was at the pump station; we talked a little bit. Daniels doing good. He is home for the summer, I guess. Ms. Thurman said he would come by before he left back for classes in the fall, I don't know if he had made it out yet?"

Rob finished the cigarette, pinching the embers between his fingers and placing the butt in his coat pocket.

The silence swallowed him whole. The wind was still quiet, it brought with it an eerie quality that floated into the atmosphere. Back at the road, cars moved in the late hour, yet the sound never reached that end of the cemetery. Crickets didn't chirp for whatever reason. No toads croaking the night away. The world felt like it pressed mute, the only sound in existence was that of Rob and him blabbing on.

Rob pressed the back of his hands against his eyes, pushing away any tears before they slipped from his eyes. He took a deep breath and tried to talk, failing to make it far enough to even utter a word.

The floodgates opened; the tears rolled out. In one moment, he had lost all composure. He began to lose his breath, gasping for air as he tried to recover. His red eyes looked up at the tombstone.

"Jed?" He managed to spit out. "Why?"

Morning came and Thursday started. Rob sat up and watched the sun slip above Bugbear Mountain. It couldn't be later than 6:30.

Rob shivered and hugged his body tight, rubbing the outside of his arms trying to warm himself up through his jacket. Rolling over he moved to his feet, brushing the dirt and dead grass from his jeans. He patted the tombstone and walked away without a word.

Reaching into his jacket, he pulled out the empty pack of reds, crumbling the box into a tight ball he dropped it into a metal trash-bin that sat on the side of the drive that ran through the grounds.

His palms placed deep into his temples, putting pressure on his head to draw back the inevitable migraine building up. His mouth was dry, he desperately needed something to drink, he smacked the mouth around, trying to roll the saliva around his mouth to moisten his tongue.

The fence was easier to climb sober, he reached up and grabbed the highest horizontal bar and lifted his body, kicking his feet out against the vertical bars and boosted himself up to the curved hooks at top. He moved his body on the hooks and simply stepped down into the tree that he used the previous night to jump into the cemetery.

Back on the ground and on the opposite side of the fence, he walked casually back to his car. The Mustang sat on the side of the road; the bright red reflected the sun as it climbed higher over the mountain. He jiggled his pockets around feeling for the keys, finding them and unlocking the door. Plopping his large body into the driver's seat.

Rob checked his wrist for the time, ten 'til seven. He opened the glove compartment and pulled out a fresh box of reds and a piece of paper. Placing the paper on his lap as he twisted off the plastic the encasing the cigarettes.

He ran his finger down the paper until he found his name, gliding it in a line until he landed on Thursday. Rob let out a huge sigh of relief as his work schedule read OFF.

The engine roared to life as he turned the key, the radio picked up where he left off, blasting The Beach Boys Good Vibrations at almost full volume. He rolled the music down halfway and pulled the car into drive.

Down the block was a convenience store, Rob dropped in and grabbed a sports drink and a travel pack of migraine relief, he tore the small package open and swallowed them before leaving the store. Rob had one particular task he wanted to complete today, and he didn't want his throbbing head to get in the way.

The first thing he needed to do was get home and shower. He could smell the whiskey seeping through his pores. The cigarettes would only mask it so much, but he wasn't sure that the smell of stale cigarettes was any better.

Three hours later, Rob parked his car in an empty parking spot at Moose Apartment Complex. He looked at himself in the mirror, straightened out his long, thin hair, and rubbed his face. Rob hadn't shaved his face in months, the skin was sore from the razor ripping the hair from his cheeks and chin. He took a deep breath and instinctively grabbed the box of cigarettes from his glove compartment, he placed a stick in his mouth and let it sit there, flicking the lighter to life and snuffing it out, flicking it to life and snuffing it out.

He watched a lady come in no hurry down the steps that lined the outside of the complex. She wore a black dress with matching heels. The dress was tight against her body, Rob admired her from the distance. She carried a small backpack around her forearm, it was overstuffed, practically bursting the zipper open.

Rob took a deep breath and counted to ten, he was never good at these types of things. Maybe, maybe he was before 5 years ago. It was possible that back then he was a decent human being though. Possible that back then, life made sense, and he was a nice man that would do nice things. He tried to remember what he was like before the loss of Jed changed everything. Most nights he wondered what life would have been like if that night Jed had stayed in that night... only a matter of minutes could have changed everything. Would he be happy? Would he still be married? Rob was sure he would be, the marriage felt rock solid up until the moment it just wasn't anymore. Most nights Rob stayed up wondering what his life could have been, it was seldom that he sat and tried to remember who he was. Maybe he wasn't a nice guy that did nice things. It's very possible he only viewed himself as a nice guy because everyone thinks they are nice and he himself wanted to believe it. All the things he had done the last 5 years, the dirty stuff, the stuff that came too easily for him, those were the things that made him think am *I fucked up* or *have I always been*?

The door shut behind him as he slowly walked away from the Mustang, the sun in the sky was bright behind him. He could turn around now, it was possible she didn't even see him or at the very least the sun made it difficult for her to see who he was.

She didn't see him, she walked over to her small orange Prius and the doors unlocked as she pulled the door. Her back was turned as Rob approached her, one hand behind his back.

He hesitated.

The moment had come, he needed to act now or walk away.

His shadow dragged long across the pavement; she could see it. She knew someone was there, the lady turned around and looked Rob square in the eyes.

A shocked look spread across the young woman's face, genuine surprise.

"Oh, my god," Becca said as her shock morphed into a smile. "Look at you?" She said, moving her arms up and down in front of Rob.

"What?" Rob said, his face turning red and hot.

"I'm impressed, I'll be honest," she said as she stepped on the tips of her toes to rub her hands against his clean cheeks, "you clean up nice."

Rob pulled his hands out from behind his back, "Here." The scent of flowers blew through the air, the breeze picked them up and it smelled like summer.

"Oh my god, Rob!" She grabbed the flowers with both hands, "You didn't have to!"

"I know."

"Well, how was your date?"

Rob shrugged his shoulders, "Didn't wake up in my bed if that means anything to ya?"

They both laughed.

"You got plans?" Becca said as her face dipped into the flowers.

"Depends on what your plans are?"

She smiled, "Okay, you wanna ride?"

Rob smiled at her and walked around to the passenger seat.

Things were easier with Becca around; she was a breath of fresh air from Rob's fucked up existence. He didn't need to be perfect with her, and he appreciated that. She knew he was troubled; she had an idea that something had happened to him in the not so distant past… she just wasn't positive to what that was. Rob made sure of that.

The night was cold, the window let the air blow through into the room with welcomed ease. Rob laid on the bed, a bed sheet barely covering his hips. He rolled over and gently kissed Becca on her bare shoulder. She made a soft sound and smiled.

"What are you thinking?" She whispered.

Rob thought about it for a moment, he had no answer. If he was thinking of anything before she asked, he couldn't recall, instead, he lied. Lying was easier for him. Lie to make someone feel better. Lie to get yourself out of whatever situation you don't want to be in.

"Just about tomorrow."

Becca rolled over, "tomorrow?"

"Yeah," he said as he rolled over, carrying the sheet with him as he did.

Becca placed a finger on his bare chest, drawing little circles, "What about tomorrow?"

"I don't know, I am just wondering what changes?"

She smiled, "What do you want to change?"

Rob rolled to his back and stared at the ceiling; the small fan rotated the air from outside at a slow pace. He thought about what she said, what did he want to change? Did he even truly know what he wanted anymore? Rob had made so many changes in his life, and if he was being honest with himself (which he never truthfully was), he didn't make those changes for him, he made it for Lanai. The lady he longed for all these years. He longed for her, as she moved on. She found herself a new man, a new life, and soon enough, she'd be having his baby. He was jealous of that man. He didn't deserve her. Rob was positive of that.

"You don't have to answer if you don't want?" The disappointment was obvious, she too rolled back around and stared at the ceiling.

"I know what I want."

"Yeah, what is that?" She rolled her head around.

"Two things."

Her entire body shifted to her side, her head propped under her arm as she looked at Rob.

"One, I don't want this night to end," he said. He waited for the thoughts to form in his head, they moved a million miles an hour but he couldn't catch any of them. "I want to wake up in the morning and have breakfast with you, but I want this night to keep going. Maybe this night can keep going for a while. Maybe that night can roll over until the next day and the next. Until one day we both wake up and realize that this night might never end."

She smiled and reached for his hand, "that doesn't sound too bad."

"Yeah," he whispered.

"What's the other thing?"

Rob hesitated for the second time that day. His brain stopped moving like a car crash on a freeway. Everything was moving as fast as possible, in a matter of a moment, everything stopped. Only one thing was on his mind, one thing was always on his mind.

"I want to see my son again."

CHAPTER SIX

The words came out without his brain giving the command. He shivered as the words slipped through his lips. For years he hadn't spoken about it. Rob went to his support group and listened, he didn't speak and after a while, that was perfectly fine with everyone. Every now and then he would give them something to go off of, but he never walked them through it.

Now, Becca gave Rob all of her focus, she sat up and leaned back against the bed frame, "What do you mean?"

Rob thought about it, the idea of letting Becca in 100% was terrifying, but something about it felt natural. It felt right.

"5 years ago, my son died in a drunk driving accident," the words slipped into the air and stood solid. The atmosphere in the room was still, neither of them took a breath.

Becca said nothing, she slipped her hand out and grabbed his. He gripped tighter than he meant to, feeling her small hand in his was a welcomed release.

"My ex-wife and I had gone to sleep some hours earlier, Jed had gone to bed before us, about 9 or so. I didn't know it, but Jed had slipped out of the house, he was going to meet some of the guys from the team for a party." Rob let go of Becca's hand, he rolled from his lying position and sat at the edge of the bed, his hands grasped through his long, thinning hair.

Becca crawled behind him, placing her arms around his waist and leaned her face on his back.

"I woke up, sometime after midnight, with the feeling that something was wrong. Lanai was dead asleep and I remember thinking felt *off*. I climbed out of bed and checked the doors, making sure they were locked. On my way back to bed I passed by Jed's room, I didn't even think to check to see if he was there."

The situation had run through Rob's mind every night for the last 5 years, every movement, every thought, every action taken in that small 5 minutes of July 13th. This was his personal hell, he kept replaying it in his head, personally torturing himself. Rob felt a tear fall loosely from his face and land on his bare chest, he used the backside of his hand and brushed his face of any remaining tears.

"I remember walking down the hallway, it was dark so it took a moment for my eyes to adjust. I had walked past Jed's bedroom, slowly walking down the hall looking at each door, peering out each window, even checking that the fucking garage door was closed. I walked back upstairs and pasted Jed's room for the second fucking time without checking. Not checking on my own fucking son."

His voice cracked, Becca was startled by it, she jumped off his back and grabbed his skin tight. Rob couldn't control his emotions anymore; everything came out between gasping breaths.

"I went back to sleep. With no problems-" Rob choked on the words for a moment before continuing. "I woke up to the doorbell a couple hours later, couldn't have been later than 1 in the morning. It was a young officer. I remember thinking he looked terrified. He told me there had been a drunk driving accident and that my son was rushed to the hospital. Some drunk fucking crashed into my son!"

Rob couldn't continue, he lost control of it and just drowned himself in tears. Grasping at Becca's arms and holding her as tight as he could.

Becca whispered into his ear, running her hand through his thin hair, "It's okay. Everything is okay."

She rocked him until he laid back down, eventually, they both fell asleep.

Friday rolled into Saturday, and Sunday, and before he knew it, the weekend had flashed in front of him.

Every day was spent with Becca, they stayed up late, too late most nights, talking (about anything but Jed). They had a bottle of wine; they drank it liberally. Buying a second bottle by Saturday.

Rob didn't care for wine, and he didn't feel the overwhelming desire to drink those nights with Becca. All this time, Rob was hiding behind the long nights at the bar or the dangerously drunk nights alone at home, and all he ever needed was someone in his life like Becca.

Sunday night, they joked and laughed, enjoying the night. The clock read eleven, but it felt so much earlier than that. They kissed and ran their hands down each others' body, stumbling down the hallway and crashing into her bed.

That night, they shared a cigarette off the balcony of Becca's apartment. Becca was wrapped up in a white robe that looked like it was completely made of towels. She disappeared inside it; her small frame tucked below the massive cover.

"I want to share something with you," she said as she blew smoke from her perfect lips. "You were brave to share with me, and I owe you the same courtesy."

Rob leaned against the railing, reaching out as she handed the burning stick, he placed it to his lips and inhaled, "I'm all yours, doll."

She smiled, not her usual smile that Rob was finding himself obsessing over, but a half-smile, something you'd give at a funeral.

"My father committed suicide when I was a teenager," she said. Her eyes looked down to her feet, her face hidden as her hair dropped over her head.

Rob dropped the cigarette in a small tray, placing his hand delicately under her chin, raising her face, "My god, I had no idea, Becca."

Becca forced another funeral-smile, "It's okay, it happened over 10 years ago."

"I'm so sorry."

"Don't be, he wasn't much of a father anyway. I mean," she stopped, her hesitation gave her eyes time to catch up with her true emotions, "I mean, he wasn't really around much."

Her beautiful blue eyes were hugged by red, she held back the tears.

Rob wrapped his large arms around her, she welcomed it, holding him too.

"I want you to know that I understand how it feels to lose someone, he wasn't my son, and I didn't love him as you did Jed, but on at least on a surface level, I get it."

Rob had heard at least 50 versions of these stories at the support group. Different people with different lives, trying to grasp at straws as they tried to relate to one another. They never seemed authentic, like they were just waiting for the next person to shut up so they had a chance to talk. To tell everyone in the room why I am important.

Becca managed to do something different. She didn't tell him everything, she didn't have to. In only a couple sentences she was able to do something that no one in the support group had been able to do before: genuinely care.

She hadn’t told him out of pity or for attention. She told him with the best intentions, and he could see it was something that was truly difficult for her to talk about. Becca seemed like an open book, but maybe she had her own chapters torn out, not available to the mass public.

Rob held her as tight as he could, kissed her on her forehead and said: “It's okay. Everything is okay.”

CHAPTER SEVEN

The months breezed by in an instant.

6 months later and Rob had moved into her apartment with her. Rob continued working at the fuel station, but he had found time to start working on graphic design again. He wasn't getting work yet, but he was happy to be working on something that made him happy. Rob didn't want to be stuck at the fuel station much longer, especially with Becca gone.

She had her first interview the Monday after she graduated and was promptly offered a job at the local hospital. It was great to see her move on from the fuel station, but ultimately, she wasn't done yet. Becca had dreamed of getting out of Linkville all her life, she was always on her phone looking for any openings in Oregon. She was excited about one job, in particular, working in Clover Cove on the coast. Becca went to her interview over a month ago, and it was the first time she didn't get a job she interviewed for. Rob thought she would have fallen apart, that maybe she'd be even slightly depressed for a moment, but she was fine. Her home wasn't in Clover Cove, it was with him.

"What are the plans tonight?" Becca asked as she picked an apple and banana out of the fruit bowl on the counter, putting them in a lunch bag.

Rob looked up from his cereal, pondered the question and answered, "What do you have in mind?"

She walked around to Rob and pushed herself between his legs, draping her small arms over his monster shoulders. She smiled as she brushed his hair from his face, "I'm going to be working pretty late, but maybe when I get off we can rent a movie and cuddle?"

Rob told her it sounded good, kissed her on the forehead and they hugged. Becca grabbed her lunch bag and he walked her to the door, kissing goodbye.

These were the times 6 months ago Rob would be at his worst. An empty apartment, no work, and all the time to overthink things and sabotage anything and everything.

But not anymore, he finished his cereal and placed the bowl in the sink. Rob flopped onto the couch that was entirely too big for only two people, grabbed the remote and flipped the television to live sports news, nothing too interesting. Nothing that required his undivided devotion.

His mind wandered, from one thing to another. He had a couple chores he wanted to accomplish today, he wanted to prep dinner so Becca would come home to a nice meal, he wanted to trim his beard... he ran his hands through his hair. It was long, it didn't have the same ratty feel it did before Becca, but it was still unappealing. He put a haircut on his to-do-list for the day.

By noon he had done the dishes, a load of laundry, cleaned up the house a bit (what he considered clean was miles away from what Becca would consider clean, but she would appreciate the effort at least). He defrosted pork chops and made sure he had all the proper ingredients for tonight's meal, noting what he needed to pick up while he was out of the house. Rob walked to the bathroom and picked up his beard trimmer, trimming it to a clean stubble. He washed his face and combed his hair, staring into the mirror as the water dripped from the faucet.

His mind wandered again, he looked into the mirror at himself.

Would he have a beard? How much would he look like me?

He pushed the thoughts from his mind, but they fought back, clawing back to the surface and choking everything else from his mind.

Would his hair be thinning by now? What would an adult Jed look like?

His pocket vibrated, breaking his train of thought, he pulled out his cell phone and flipped it open.

I love you, the message from Becca said.

Rob smiled and responded: I love you more.

After his haircut, he swung by the grocery store and grabbed a couple items, walking a bit out of his way to the wine section tucked away in the back corner of the store.

He found that he enjoyed a glass of wine occasionally, something that he previously couldn't stand. At first, Becca was terrified that any kind of alcohol would be a bad idea, but Rob wasn't. He didn't want to lose her. He wouldn't lose her. Rob knew that he only drank to mask his pain, but with Becca, he had no pain. Most of the time anyway.

"Rob?" A voice asked from behind him.

He turned around and saw Marla, a shopping cart in front of her. She looked the same as usual, her hair was still pulled back into a ponytail, her face still carried the same cautious smile as she looked at him. Marla wore a long red jacket that hung low to her knees.

"Oh my gosh?" She said with a smile as she left her cart and walked towards him. "How have you been?"

Rob wrapped her into his arms, hugging her in a way that even surprised himself, "I've been good. Real good."

"Yeah?" She said as she pulled off him, "We haven't seen you for a while."

"I know, I kind of moved on from the group."

"I noticed."

"Things have finally started making sense again, I'm finding a way to be happy again."

"That's great, Rob. I'm so happy to hear it."

Smiles were exchanged as the small talk came to a natural end. Marla recommended the right bottle of wine and they hugged again before saying goodbye.

"I'm really proud of you, Rob. If you found a way to be happy again, anyone can. Maybe come by one of these nights and help someone else?"

"Maybe."

The clinks of empty plates being placed into the sink, Rob turned on the water and scrubbed the dishes as Becca finished her glass of wine and continued the conversation from dinner.

"I'm just over him," she said. "He can be such a jackass."

"Sorry, Bec."

She leaned against the kitchen counter and sipped the wine, "It's not your fault. I just get so sick of some of the people, it makes it hard to want to go there most of the time."

"Have you given up on the search for greener pastures?"

A short silence rose from the question, Becca sipped her glass and formed her answer carefully, "I mean, I think I have for now."

Rob turned the water off, drying his hands with a kitchen towel, "Why is that?"

Becca finished the wine and placed the glass in the sink, "You know why?"

"I told you to not pass up an opportunity because of me, haven't I?"

"I haven't passed on anything, but that doesn't mean I want to look either."

"You haven't passed on anything?"

"Nope," she said with a smile as she slowly approached him, placing her hand on his chest.

"Clover Cove?" He said looking down at her.

"What about it?"

"You are going to tell me they didn't offer you a job? I find that hard to believe."

Becca didn't respond.

"That's what I thought."

"They didn't offer me a job, Rob," her voice was defensive. "I think in a couple years when I have gotten some experience under my belt, I could get on... but it wasn't meant to be."

"Or was it not meant to be, because you know I'm not going?"

"What does that mean?"

"You know what that means."

Becca patted his chest and pushed away, walking into the living room.

"Becca, I'm not leaving Linkville. I have told you that all along," Rob said as he followed her.

"You could if you wanted. You could," she said, her eyes red as tears began to form.

Rob sat down on the couch, patting the cushion for her to join him.

"I want to, I do. But I can't.

"Rob," she said. "You can. He would want you to."

"He doesn't get a say in this," Rob fired back.

"Move on," Becca said softly. "Move on with me."

"What? How could you say that?"

"I want to have a life with you, Rob. To build a future with you, but you will always push away. I can't sit around and wait. Move on. You deserve to be happy."

Rob stood up and moved to the coat closet, grabbing a jacket and reaching for his car keys from the usual spot on the shelf.

"I'm sorry, that came out wrong. I've had too much wine," she said. "Please come back."

Rob slammed the door as he left.

CHAPTER EIGHT

Loggers Tavern hadn't changed in the last 6 months. Depressingly, it clung on to its image so it would fit its patrons. The smell was still thick with cigarette smoke and old beer.

Rob sat at his usual spot, rubbing his hands over his face as he waited for Carol to make her way in his direction.

"Well, hello," she said with a friendly smile. "Whiskey?"

Rob smiled and nodded. He pulled his cell phone from his pocket and checked the messages.

Carol brought back the whiskey, putting it on a disposable coaster in front of him. "How has life been?"

Rob brought the drink to his lips, "I'm here ain't I?"

"Point taken."

"You ever wonder if you are doomed to be miserable? Like nothing in your life, even when things are at its best, is going to ever be right? I have everything going for me, for the first time in a long fucking time. Still, here I am."

Carol poured more whiskey into his quickly empty glass, "You'll be fine. Unless you've found a different shithole to be hanging out in for the last couple months, I would say that you have found something that makes you happy. Everything will be fine, kid."

She smiled at him again and moved on back down the bar.

"Hey, buddy!" The voice shot the hairs on the back of Rob's neck up like rockets.

"No," Rob said as the taller ginger walked up to him.

"Been a while? How are things?" Eric asked as he sipped water from a glass.

"I'm meeting someone, please leave."

"I'll keep you company until he shows up. How about that?" Eric said as a question, but Rob knew there was no way out of it.

"How is life treating ya?" Eric said.

"Good," Rob said.

"Me too. I've been doing very good actually," Eric answered the question Rob didn't ask.

"If you are doing so *good*, than why would you be here?"

Eric froze for a moment, before chuckling to himself and patting Rob on the back.

"You get it, man you are really fast," Eric said.

"Yup, that's me. A wise motherfucker."

"But, if I might ask, why would you be here?"

"Eric, my friend is here. It's time for you to leave," Rob said pointing away.

Across the room, a short man entered. He kept both his hands in the pockets of his jacket, he looked around the bar. He was clearly uncomfortable; he didn't want to be here.

Rob waved him over.

"Oh, cool. Well, have a great night, Rob," Eric said as he left.

The short man sat beside Rob at the bar, ordered a beer and turned to Rob.

"Who was that?" he asked.

"Nobody," Rob said.

"You've been ducking me," he said.

"Sorry, David, I know it's been kind of a dick move."

"No shit," David said as he motioned his arms for them to move to a small table away from the bar, more private.

"I called, I texted, I even went to your apartment for a while. Eventually, I gave up. I figured I'll hear from you when I hear from you. Then tonight, Boom, text from you."

"Yeah, it's been different."

"How so?"

Rob filled him in on the last 6 months. About Becca and all the amazing things she had brought with her. Someone that was happy to see him, to talk to him, to bring him back from the brink of nothingness. Becca had seen him for more than what he had and had elevated him to get there again. He owed everything to Becca, and that's why he needed to talk to David.

"I need your help," Rob finally admitted.

David looked at him, waiting for the follow-up.

"How'd you do it?" Rob mumbled before he took a sip from his glass.

"Excuse me?"

"How'd you do it? You know, after Penny?"

"I don't think I'm following you, Robby?"

Rob finished the glass and fumbled in his pockets for a cigarette, "I'm sorry, I know this is random and kinda fucked."

"How long do we go back?" David asked as Rob at last managed to pull out a cigarette and light it.

A deep inhale later, "10 or so years?"

"We've been through a lot together, yeah? I'm here for you, always have been. What are you getting at, Rob?"

"I'm not ready for someone like Becca. I want to be. So bad. You know, but, I'm just not ready for it. I'm not ready to move on just yet."

The pieces came together, David nodded and sipped from his beer.

"When your wife died from cancer, we had just met. I remember it. You were sad, sure, but you seemed to pick your life up pretty fast afterward. Part of me always thought it was for the boys' sake, maybe you needed to be strong for them and not let Penny's death be the end of you and the boys' life too. But, how did you do it?"

David sat there quiet. He picked up his beer and sipped it, setting it back down and picking it back up again. His eyes squinted at Rob, focusing on his eyes.

"I'm sorry man, that was stupid. I'm just not sure what to do and it was wrong of me to come at you like this," Rob apologized.

David placed the empty beer bottle on the table, dug into his back pocket and retrieved his wallet, "Don't be sorry." He pulled out a hundred and put it by the bottle. "Drink."

"What?" Rob looked at his only remaining friend confused. He tried to think back to when he first met David and the David that came after Penny's death. Rob didn't remember a single time David was drunk; he didn't mask his pain in alcohol. Not the way Rob had done for so much of the last 5 years.

"Drink as much as you need to," David said. "If you still want to ask me, I'll be at the fountain in the park."

"Why do I need to be drunk first?"

David patted his friend on the shoulder, "Trust me, you'll want to be."

Rob walked the path 3 hours later, drunk enough to walk straight, but only barely.

He made his way as the path curved through the park; the large trees covered him from the night sky. The moon was large, illuminating everything as if it was a street light.

"Drunk enough?" David yelled from the fountain as Rob approached.

"I guess we'll see, won't we," Rob responded.

"Where's my change?"

Rob shrugged.

"You drank $100 worth of alcohol in a couple hours?"

"I did not," Rob said with a smile. "But Carol got one hell of a tip."

"You're a dick," David said as he walked over to a bench and patted it for Rob to join him.

Rob sat down and waited, looking down to his small friend, waiting for him to start. David watched the fountain as the water shot up from the base. It was a decent sized fountain for such a small town, it was a memorial for one of the citizens that disappeared crab fishing so many years ago. Their boat disappeared at sea. It was big news at the time, people claimed it was the Bermuda triangle, only the ship was last heard of south of Alaska.

"What would you do to see your loved one again?" David said.

Rob waited.

"That's what I was asked, after Penny's funeral."

"I don't get it."

"You will, and you won't. Just wait," David said. "It was her great-uncle or something like that, I had only met the man at the funeral so that tells you how important in her life he was. He walked up to me, caught me throwing back some jack and asked me that question."

Rob was silent.

"He asked me the question and walked away. A couple of weeks later, there was a knocking at the door and guess who it was? I had been drinking every moment of those days in between. Guilty in my heart that I couldn't function as a father, but I was just so dead inside. I needed it; you get that though."

Rob lowered his head.

"Her great-uncle asked me again, 'What would you do to see your loved one again'? I remember wanting to punch him in the face, kicking him while he was trying to get up, stomping his old body to the ground... but I couldn't. I began to cry. The truth was I would do anything to see her again. I invited him in and he told me what I'm about to tell you. And I was just the right amount of drunk to believe him."

Silence swept over the men as they sat on the bench, the wind blew the branches of the trees above, the smell of pine flew through the air. Lingering like a perfume from a mistress.

"There is a way to see your loved ones again after they'd passed. But it isn't to be taken lightly, it isn't for the faint of heart, and it most certainly isn't for the weak. It's evil."

"Bullshit," Rob couldn't hide the anger in his voice.

"No, you asked. I'm telling you the truth."

"So, after Penny died, she came back from the dead? She was cremated you fucking asshole."

"It doesn't work that way, she's not a zombie you moron. Just fucking listen and maybe you'll understand."

Rob rolled his eyes and leaned back into the bench, crossing his arms dramatically like a teenager.

"You can exchange the life of a loved one with someone else. You see, Penny was already dead, so someone had to take her place. I had to find someone, anyone really, and damn their soul to hell in exchange for seeing my wife again. The memory is vivid. I replay it in my head every night."

"What are you saying? You cursed someone?"

"No, Robby, I'm saying I killed someone! I went out one night and hunted down this kid. He didn't even know I was there until my buck knife was 3 inches into his chest," David leaned into his back pocket and again pulled out his wallet. He opened it up and pulled out a newspaper clipping, he unfolded it and handed it to Rob.

"That dude that went missing out in the woods?" Rob raised an eyebrow.

David nodded his head.

"Nope, I remember this guy. It was before I moved here, probably 3 or 4 months, they found his body slumped over at the base of a tree. He shot himself in the foot and couldn't get back before he bled to death."

David looked up at him, his eyes cloudy with tears, "Yeah."

"This doesn't add up, sorry."

A creepy smile crawled across David's face, "How so?"

"First of all, you didn't kill him, he killed himself by being an idiot. Second of all, Penny was still alive for another 5, maybe 6 months after they found his body."

David took a moment, wiped the tear that ran down his cheek. "Penny died from breast cancer October

6th, a couple weeks later, her great-uncle told me how to bring her back, it was a couple months after that until I went through with it."

"The person I sacrificed swapped places with Penny. He took her place in the timeline that was already set up. I woke up the next morning and Penny was laying beside me in our bed as if nothing had happened. For her, nothing had happened."

Rob shook his head in disbelief, opened his mouth as David continued.

"It was almost Halloween, which means that the world never skipped a beat. She remembered everything from October 6th until the morning we woke up. The world kept chugging along and I just jumped into the new world. I had to catch up with it."

"Why did Penny still die?" Rob asked, his voice was almost sarcastic.

"You exchange a soul for a soul, but it isn't permanent. It was like living on borrowed time, she had an expiration date. I lived every fucking second with her, in fear of the moment it happened again. But I took advantage of it. We vacationed. We laid in bed longer. We made love longer. When it inevitably happened again, February 2nd, I accepted it. I was able to pick the boys up with me and we continued to live."

"I don't understand why you're telling me this?" Rob said softly. "Why you would go through all this trouble to make up such a disgusting lie."

David shrugged, "Maybe that's your answer. Why would I make this up?"

"I don't know."

"Robby, listen to me. You asked me a question, I told you the truth. I've never told anyone the truth. I killed a man. Some punk from Minnesota named Jacob. I found him drunk at a bar and followed him, hunted him and killed him in the bushes behind us. I have to live with that for the rest of my life," David paused. "I'm not telling you to do it, I exchanged one pain for another. All I'm saying is that there is another choice."

Rob stood up from the bench, paced back and forth from the fountain to the bench. "I'm not saying I believe you, because it's fucking crazy, but out of interest... how did you do it?"

The creepy smile returned to David's face, "Pick someone, anyone. It doesn't matter how you do it, but you need their blood after they have died. The blood needs to be placed to the earth and you need to say this exactly: blood for blood, a life for a life. In exchange for what's been done, return a loved one."

"Then?"

"Wake up the next morning in a new world, in your case a world where Jed lived an extra 5 years at least."

"That's it?"

"Yup."

"No lightning? No explosions? The devil didn't reach from the ground and rip the soul from the dead person?"

"This isn't Hollywood, Rob. Go to sleep and wake up happy."

Rob stopped pacing, he looked over at David, "Do you regret it?"

"No. I did a horrible thing, but for a bit longer with Penny. If I could go back in time, I wouldn't talk myself out of it."

Rob nodded and patted his friend on the back, he turned around and walked back towards the tavern.

"Rob?"

He stopped.

"What would you do to see your loved one again?"

"Anything."

CHAPTER NINE

Rob stumbled from the bar as Carol walked him out, offering to fetch him a taxi, he kindly declined and said goodbye. He fumbled for his keys for a moment, deciding if he should hoof it home or not.

A couple calming breaths later, Rob moved to his car and unlocked the door. He turned the ignition and rolled the volume down. If he was going risk driving home drunk, he would at least try to not be distracted by the melodic tunes of the beach boys.

The streets were bare, it was midnight on a Saturday night, this part of town wasn't usually popping anyhow. Rob rolled down the street, careful to stay focused on his cruising speed and staying within his lane.

Soon enough he would be in bed with Becca, he would climb in beside her and kiss the back of her neck. Tomorrow morning he would nurse his hangover and cook them breakfast to the best of his abilities. Rob would apologize and hope she forgave him.

The Mustang came to a stop at a red light.

The conversation with David crept into his mind. It was crazy. Maybe that was why David wanted Rob drunk? In his state he would listen to a lot of bullshit that had he been sober, he would have scuffed at and walked away. David killed someone, or at least claimed he did, for Penny. Could he do the same for Jed?

Rob shook the thought from his head. No, it wasn't true. Rob would do anything to see his son again. To hold hug him. Talk to him. Be with him again. He wanted nothing more to just see his smile and hear his laugh.

The light turned green and Rob rolled his car forward, picking up speed as he was lost in his thoughts.

The thought of Jed, 20 going on 21. A grown man. Sharing a beer with him as they watched the Niners on a Sunday.

In a split second, the Mustang jumped the curb and bounced onto the sidewalk. Rob snapped from his daydream and swung the wheel as the car cut sharply from the sidewalk, out of control.

The car spun over the opposite lane and bounced onto the neighboring sidewalk. Rob caught a glimpse of a horrified face as it disappeared below the car, the car bumped over it and came to a stop.

Rob sat behind the wheel, eyes wide.

What have I done?

He opened the door and went to the front of the Mustang, the cherry-red hood was caked with a fresh deeper red. It dripped from the hood over the grill.

Rob turned around and his fears came to life, an unmoving figure sprawled 20 feet behind his car.

He sprinted to the figure and came to a stop only a foot in front of it.

Her beautiful blonde hair now soaked red, sprawled over a nice bright red jacket.

Rob recognized that jacket.

He rolled her over, looking into the scratched and bleeding face of Marla.

"Oh, fuck," Rob said.

He reached over and pushed his fingers to her neck.

A pulse.

Rob stood up and reached into his pocket feeling for his phone, he pulled it out and as fast as he could keyed in 9-1-1.

He stopped. No one was around. He looked at the surrounding businesses, the majority were shady, the kind that populated this part of town. They wouldn't have security cameras. The traffic lights might have cameras in them, but he wasn't sure.

He felt her pulse again.

"Shit," he said as he ran his fingers through his long, thinning hair. "Shit. Shit. Shit."

Rob reached his giant hands and over her bloody face, covering her mouth and nose.

An eternity went by as Rob checked with his free hand her pulse until there appeared to be nothing.

"I'm sorry. I'm sorry. I'm sorry," Rob wept as he kept the pressure on her face. After a few more minutes, Rob rubbed his hand through her bloody hair.

He crawled over to a large potted plant that stood outside one business and tipped it over. The plant and soil scattered on the ground.

"Blood for blood. Life for a life. In exchange for what's been done, return a loved one."

Rob slammed his foot on the gas as hard as he could, the car screamed off the sidewalk and tore down the road.

He kept his eyes on the rearview mirror until he no longer could make out Marla's lifeless body. With both hands on the wheel, he concentrated on the road. What had he just done? Why did he do it? She could have lived, could have made it! He should have finished dialing 9-1-1 and gotten her help. He always had a feeling that Marla was terrified of him, and maybe she had every right to be. Why was she even on this part of town this time of the night?

Rob thought about it a moment and realized it was Saturday night, she was leaving the late-night session at the church. She was helping people like she always did. Marla didn't deserve to die, not like that.

Shaking, Rob grabbed for his cigarettes, before seeing headlights coming down the street towards him. He straightened up and put both hands back on the wheel. He calmed himself and took several deep breaths.

Everything is going to be alright, he reassured himself.

The car passed him, Rob tried to pay attention to the car, but it was too dark and he was going too fast to see anything but a dark car pass by.

"Fuck!" Rob screamed as he looked down at his speedometer, he was so nervous about the car he forgot to adjust his speed.

He looked through his mirror again to see the car flip around and follow behind him, gaining speed before flipping on the red and blue lights.

Rob cursed again, pressing his foot as hard down as he could.

The Mustang ripped down the road, Rob watched his speedometer climb to 80.

How did this happen? He wanted to fix his life with Becca, find a way to make a life with her. He wanted to get as much help as he could from David, maybe fix himself and make his existence less of a mess. Rob finally felt like his life was making sense again, Becca loved him in a way he never felt with his ex-wife. She was the only thing that managed to bring him back from the brink. Why did he fuck everything up? Why did he need to solve his problems at the bottom of another bottle?

The cruiser matched his speed as the barreled down the road, turning a hard right, which Rob did not adjust his speed for.

Rob watched as the cruiser slowed down on the turn, his marginal lead was extended. He pushed the car further as he climbed off the main street and up an on-ramp. Once on top of the ramp, Rob rolled the wheel turning the car down oncoming traffic.

Luckily, few cars were on the highway, making it easy for Rob to weave between them as he pushed the car past 100. He looked behind him and saw as the cruiser pulled off the ramp, following the flow of traffic.

Rob continued to drive like a confused foreigner down the highway, lucky for him the small town didn't have a large amount of law enforcement and for the time being, he seemed to be in the clear.

How many cherry-red mustangs were in town though? Rob could only think of 3 off the top of his head, that wouldn't make it too hard to track him and the car down. If he managed to make it home, he was positive he would wake up the next morning to policemen at his door.

He reached over to his cup holder which he had placed his cell in. Rob debated if he should call Becca, tell her everything. He couldn't do that though. Maybe he could just tell her how important he was to him? Rob looked at the time displayed on his stereo, it's too late, she would be dead asleep, he didn't want to leave a voicemail.

Up ahead there would be an off ramp, he knew it would turn down Greensprings Blvd. He could disappear in there; the small neighborhood was infested with back roads and dirt-roads that led out of view.

Rob pushed past another car, how many cars had he passed in only a few minutes going the opposite way down the highway? 6 maybe 7? How many of them would call the authorities? Shit, how did that not occur to him already? Rob looked in his rearview mirror again as a blue and red flashing light twinkled to life in the distance.

So much for him disappearing.

Rob kept climbing his speed to 120, faster than he had ever taken the mustang before.

He could see the Greensprings exit ahead, there was still time to make the turn and disappear. If he could zip into the neighborhood fast enough, it's possible with the distance between them that the officer wouldn't even see him make the turn.

Rob turned his headlights off, if he was able to sneak the turn, the headlights would surely give it away.

The highway disappeared in a blink, the lights that hung above the highway stretched few and far between. Maneuvering the road would be difficult, but with the moon out it was almost possible.

Rob adjusted the mirror, trying to locate the cruiser sprinting towards him. The mirror dropped, settling on the backseat. Rob's heart dropped as a figure appeared in the backseat, he could see the outline partially blocking the back window.

He focused his attention on the road, Rob didn't realize how far he had drifted in the few seconds he looked away.

Rob tried to fight the urge, but he couldn't. He grabbed the mirror again and pushed it to the empty back seat.

"Holy hell," he pushed out. He didn't even notice he had been holding his breath in the process.

The mustang flew past another light as he lowered his hand from the mirror, the light illuminated the passenger seat.

Sitting beside him was a beautiful blonde in a large red jacket.

Rob's eyes grew large as he could see the fresh blood drip from Marla's hair to the shoulder of her jacket. He looked at hands that were placed on her lap, her dress was pulled up and Rob could see the ripped open thigh deep to the bone, blood overflowing and filling her lap like a kiddie pool. Her fingers were otherwise fine, except the middle finger no longer had the cheap red nail she was known for.

THUD, THUD, THUD, THUD, THUD. Rob adjusted the wheel as he unknowingly had drifted off the highway momentarily.

Rob flew past his exit; every inch of his concentration was focused on Marla. She made a wretched sound as blood mixed in her lungs. Her breathing sounded like she was gargling water.

Marla began to turn towards him, for the first time he stared into her eyes. He could see the deadness of her eyes, the fog that rolled over her usual blue eyes. The right side of her face was swollen and broken; he could see the jaggedness of the broken bone trying to pop through her eye socket.

In a flash Marla lunged out of her seat and pounced Rob, he threw his arms up in self-defense, dropping the wheel right as he did so.

The mustang going over 120 MPH jumped off the highway, slamming into the guard rail that snapped like a matchstick between two thumbs. The car flew through the air, corkscrewing until it slammed to the ground nose first. Rob felt the sudden impact as his body was ejected from the car through the door window, his body a rag doll as it flopped through the air.

CHAPTER TEN

Rob sprung from his bed; the morning sun shined brightly from the large bedroom window. Rob struggled to catch his breath, his heart beat as if he had chugged a pot of coffee and washed it down with a couple energy drinks. A single eyebrow raised as he noticed the window, the curtains that were pulled neatly to each side of the window were different. He looked around and noticed that everything was different. His bedding was a thick winter comforter that was better suited for the Oregon winter than his thin 49er throw blanket that usually adorned his bed. The bed sat on top of a large frame that monstered over his head. He reached to the nightstand and retrieved his phone, which was in a black charging dock, along with an iPad and his wallet.

He tossed the phone around in his hand a couple times. Was it his phone? It was on his nightstand but it was a lot nicer than the one he was used to. He pressed the home button to the lock screen and punched in the same password he had since he was a teenager. It worked.

Rob sat up and noticed his slippers tucked under his feet, he slid them on and walked over to what he assumed was a closet. He opened the door, pulled out a bathrobe hooked to the inside of the door. Inside the closet he saw his clothes hung on the left side with care, his shoes were stacked in a row below his shirts, instead of in a pile below a mountain of discarded shirts and pants. On the right side of the closet, he noticed someone else's clothes, dresses, and blouses. He grabbed the nearest one, a bright blue cocktail dress.

It was Lanai's. She wore it the night he proposed to her over a decade ago.

"It worked," the words slipped from his mouth. A smile emerged as the words activated his brain as it put all the pieces together.

It must have worked. If Jed never died, then he wouldn't have started to drink. If he didn't start to drink, he wouldn't have slipped into a deep depression. He wouldn't have lost his job. He wouldn't have lost his wife. They had planned to build a house if their finances ever made it feasible. Apparently, it had.

Rob walked out of the bedroom and down a hall, a large open staircase at the end of the hall was lined with framed pictures.

He paused at each new one.

A picture of Jed in his high school basketball uniform, posed with a basketball tucked under his arm.

A picture with him in a tux, his arm wrapped around a short girl with a bright red dress. The backdrop was a silhouette of buildings, a large starlit night behind that. Jed smiled large with a matching red top-hat. The bottom of the picture read: PROM 2017. His senior prom.

Picture after picture filled in the life that Jed should have had. A large grid of pictures from his graduation, him holding a diploma, posing with his friends, posing with Rob and Lanai. Another picture of the three of them rafting. One of Jed holding the keys to the Mustang, the interior of the Mustang was packed full of balloons, one of which had the numbers 16 centered.

"Holy balls, I gave him the Mustang," Rob said with a smile.

The information overload was welcomed, but he was ready to move on. There was always another time he could catch up on the fine details.

He moved down the stairs and heard the faint sound of music, he followed the sound to the kitchen.

Lanai grabbed a piece of toast from a plate and took a bite, she jammed to her usual 90s playlist that echoed from a small speaker in the corner of the large kitchen.

She smiled at him, finished chewing and walked over to him, kissing him on the cheek. "Morning, sleepy." She moved past him and grabbed a travel mug, filling it with coffee and creamer.

"Morning," Rob said.

"I was wondering if you were planning on waking up? Running a little late?"

Rob walked over to a basket of fruit, thumbed through it and grabbed a green apple, shined it on his sleeve and bit into it.

"Have you talked to Jed today?" A piece of apple popped from his mouth as he chewed. He smiled and wiped his face, "Sorry."

Lanai opened the refrigerator door and ducked her head inside, "Um, no, why?"

"Just curious, haven't talked to him in a while."

She closed the door and held out a lunch pail Rob immediately recognized, the silver glitter didn't look as new as it once did, he smiled to himself when he realized she still had the same lunch pail through all these years. "So how long is a while? You guys talked last night?"

"I mean," Rob tried to think of a good lie, nothing came to mind.

"You gonna get ready for work?" Lanai asked as she looked at her watch, taking another bite from her toast.

Rob leaned back against the counter, took another bite from his apple and pulled out his phone. "I was thinking of playing hooky today."

"Yeah?" Lanai smiled and walked up to him, he wrapped his arms around her.

"Yeah, I figured I could catch up on some of the work around here and maybe relax."

"Doesn't sound like a bad idea, maybe next time give me a proper warning and I could skip work with you," she winked.

They kissed. It was just as he remembered. It sparked everything he missed about her. Their first kiss. Their first vacation together, to an old lake house off the coast. To the night Rob got down on one knee and asked the big question.

Everything came flooding back, but it felt foreign. It felt off, by a degree or two.

"Alright, I'm off," she said. "I'll call you on my lunch. Try to get some rest." She planted another kiss on his cheek and blew him a kiss as she left.

Rob moved to the living room and plopped down on a familiar couch, "Finally, something we didn't replace."

He dug into his robe and pulled out his phone, thumbed through the contacts. His thumb hovered over the name Jed for too long, he was hesitant to press it. Nerves were getting the better of him.

Something moved out of the corner of his eye, past the room down the hallway.

Rob peered his head as far as he could, he couldn't see anybody.

He peeled the curtains in the living room back, he watched as Lanai's car fully emerged from their driveway and pulled down the street.

Still, something had caught his attention. Rob stood up and looked further down the hall, following it to a shut door.

Between the floor and the bottom of the door, a light flicked on. Rob took a step back, the suddenness of it shocked him. The doorknob made a popping sound as it jumped open an inch, exposing the light from inside, casting a beam down the otherwise dim hallway.

CREEAK.

The door crawled open; Rob couldn't move. His brain was telling him something was wrong, but his body couldn't do anything but watch.

After a couple inches, the door stopped. The light inside flickered, off and on. The light flickered faster and faster until it was as rapid as a strobe light.

Another sudden noise made Rob step back, a heavy BANG.

Slowly, on the floor, something appeared from the edge of the doorway. Rob squinted as he tried to see what it was. It was dark and thick, crawling out like a living creature.

Blood.

Within seconds the blood oozed out, pushing the door further open revealing the bathroom with the strobing lights.

The walls were thick with blood, it streamed down the walls from the roof. The sink was on, blood poured out the faucet like a sadistic waterfall. It overflowed the bowl and splashed to the ground.

Blood made no noise as it poured to the ground, Rob noticed a slight hum that began to get louder and louder until it was all he could hear.

The blood made its way to his slippers, he noticed too late, the thick blood clung to his slippers. He stepped back and a fresh bloody print lifted from his slipper.

The humming got louder, he grabbed both his ears to block the noise out.

His hand buzzed; he pulled the phone in front of his eyes to see Lanai was calling him.

He pulled the phone away. Everything was back to normal. The floor was clean, his slippers were dry, the bathroom door was closed.

Rob moved to the bathroom, opening it up as he answered the call.

The bathroom was empty, cleaned to a degree that only Lanai could have done it.

"Hello?" He mumbled.

"Hey, just calling to remind you that if you do talk to Jed, please ask him if he was bringing his girlfriend to dinner this weekend when he comes to town?"

"Um, of course," he said as he pulled the door closed. "Yeah, no problem."

Rob moved to the kitchen sink and threw cold water on his face, rubbing his eyes deep.

"Fuck," he whispered.

He turned back towards the bathroom, pausing for something to happen. After a minute, nothing had happened, and Rob decided he needed to get dressed. More likely he decided he needed to get away from the bathroom door before it opened again.

He moved up the stairs and brought his phone out again, pressed on Jed's name and brought it to his ear. Rob paused at the top of the stairs and waited as the phone rang. After a couple rings it was interrupted by an automated voicemail asking to leave a message, Rob thought about it momentarily, deciding to hang up and call again. The phone rang even shorter this time before it went again to the automated voicemail.

The phone buzzed, he looked at the face as a new text message popped up. He clicked it.

The message was from Jed, "Sup? Can't talk, in class."

Rob smiled, thought about his response and typed back: "Hey, I have a meeting in your area this afternoon... lunch?"

He waited for a response. He wished he could have heard his voice, he missed it most.

The phone buzzed again, "Sure. Phones gonna die. Meet me at my apartment when you get here. Loves."

"Loves."

Rob got dressed, a clean gray shirt and khaki shorts. Moved to the bathroom to comb his hair, his eyes dropped as he stood at the mirror.

"My hair?" His voice was shocked as he ran his hand over his bald head. "When? Why?" His mouth hung open as he rubbed the bare skin, "Dammit."

That wasn't the only difference he noticed, his beer belly was gone. His large frame didn't carry the weight of the half-decade of alcohol and self-neglect. His clothes didn't smell like cigarettes either, he probably hadn't smoked since high school once again.

Rob moved back downstairs, grabbing a lonely set of keys from a hook by the door. He turned back down the hallway, keeping an eye on the bathroom door as he picked his pace to a brisk walk past the door and through the only remaining door in the hallway.

Once in the garage, he looked at his new vehicle. A black Mustang, no more than 4 years old.

He climbed in the driver seat, pressing the garage door opener on the visor. He popped the address into the GPS, he had asked Lanai for the address once he got off the phone with Jed. She asked what he needed it for, he told her he was going to send him a package that he needed before the weekend.

Rob looked through his phone for the contact that read Work, clicked it and called it while his phone connected to the Bluetooth on his car.

"Morning, Rob," a younger female voice said. Rob double checked his phone at the number he called. He didn't work at Tyler's Friendly Pump anymore, the thought of it excited him.

"Hey, sorry, I'm not gonna make it in today," he said.

"Oh, I figured as much since you are over an hour late," the voice sound playfully. "I already rescheduled your meetings for tomorrow, don't make me do it again."

"Deal," he said. "See ya tomorrow."

He hung up the phone, he rubbed his cheeks on both sides. They were sore, he hadn't smiled so much in the morning for as long as he could remember. This was what his life was supposed to be. He loved every moment of it.

The 3-hour drive from Linkville to Eugene was the longest drive of Rob's life. He kept reminding himself of what was just down the road, Jed.

To pass the time, Rob had picked up his phone and scrolled through his contacts, he wanted to get some questions answered, one thing in particular... The visions. He knew there was only one person who could answer his questions. Rob scrolled alphabetically; the contacts read "Darren" to "Dean". He moved to the last names, maybe he had labeled David by his last name? Still no luck.

Rob moved on, still, some particular questions plagued his mind. What happened in his bathroom this morning? Why was David not in his contacts? Was Jed going to die again? That last question stung the worst. He wasn't ready for it to happen. Penny had lived for a couple months before she died again, but that was from cancer. Once she came back, she was still sick. Regardless, her body would give out. Maybe things could be different with Jed. Maybe this time he won't be swept away by a drunk in a bronco.

Cars flew by, Rob's attention shifted like the gears of the Mustang. Suddenly his mind glided back to the previous night. Less than 12 hours ago he had clasped his hands tight around someone's face, making sure she wouldn't breathe again. He would jump in his car and flee from the police, ending flipped in a ditch. Did he die in that car?

Probably, he was rolling over 120 mph. It seemed impossible he would have survived. Why was he alive? Maybe he died? Maybe this is all a dream? Or worse yet, maybe this is all a nightmare?

Is this hell? Rob rolled the thought around in his head. If this was hell, he imagined it a much worse scene.

Rob looked over at the passenger seat, it was still empty. Cautiously, he looked to the rearview mirror. A wave of relief rushed over him as he looked at an empty back seat.

He looked back up, noticing that the car in front of him was closer than he remembered. He slowed his car, looking down at the speedometer.

120.

"Whoa," he said to himself. Slowing down as fast as he could, but not fast enough as the car in front of him grew closer by the second. He swerved into the next lane, close to colliding with another vehicle in the process. The tires squealed as he pulled the wheel hard to avoid a collision.

Finally, the car was free of any vehicles, his speed approached an acceptable limit.

Rob brushed the sweat from his forehead, pressing the cruise control on the steering wheel.

"Align with the right lane, your exit is coming up," his GPS announced.

Rob moved down the street, approaching Jed's apartment. The GPS announced his arrival at his destination, he found an empty parking spot on the street kitty-corner of Jed's complex.

Rob opened the door and stretched. He grabbed his phone from the cupholder and exited the vehicle. Rob messaged Jed, letting him know he had made it, hoping that his phone would have charged since the last time they talked.

Scouting the parking lot, Rob was able to pick out the only cherry-red mustang. He walked through the lot, one step closer to seeing his son again.

The neighborhood was decent enough, he noticed that there were a couple minivans parked in the parking lot, there were probably a couple families in the complex. He looked around at the surrounding houses, all the houses seemed to be maintained. Nothing too alarming, Jed had picked a nice neighborhood as far as he was concerned.

As he approached his old Mustang, something caught his attention. The grill was folded in, the hood was a dented mess. He picked up his pace, covering the ground at a mild jog. The closer he got, the more obvious it became, the car looked like it had just hit someone.

It did.

Marla.

Blood oozed from the grill, falling to the ground. Clunks of hair wedged in between the folds. The front half of the hood was showered in a deep, dark red.

Rob approached the vehicle, placing a hand on the hood. He looked at the palm of his hand, it was dry.

He looked back at the front of the car, nothing but a little dirt. No damage. It was in need of a wash, but nothing you wouldn't expect of a college student. Rob took a step back and brushed the dirt on his shirt. Rob took a step back and tried to run his hands through his hair, only to be surprised by his baldness once again.

"Hey!" He heard from behind him.

Rob turned around and saw Jed waving from a balcony that led to stairs.

Rob froze.

He wanted to move, he wanted to run towards his son and lift him in the air like he did when he was younger. Raise him high and then bring him in for a tight hug, hold him for as long as he could before he squirmed his way away from his grasp. Rob couldn't move. He was paralyzed. Not with fear, but relief.

This wasn't a nightmare. No, this was real. Jed was truly alive; he was walking towards him.

"How's it going, old man?" Jed said with a smile. His voice was deeper than Rob expected. He was an adult.

Rob watched him walk, even his gait was different. He strode with all the unearned confidence of a young adult, powerful and with a purpose.

Jed wore dark green sweatpants, his college logo emblazoned on the leg. He wore a tight-fitting sweatshirt, gray with the college name centered.

His hair was shaggy, rolling over his ears. His smile was from ear to ear, a hint of facial hair growing from his chin.

"Where do you want to eat?" Jed said.

Rob smiled, opened his mouth to answer.

BANG!

CHAPTER ELEVEN

Rob opened his eyes.

Lanai stood up and ran to his side, her makeup was chaos with black streaks down her face. She looked like she hadn't slept in years. She looked just like she did 5 years ago.

"What's going on?" Rob said, his voice was raspy.

"Everything is going to be okay," she assured him. She squeezed his hand, tighter and tighter. "You got out of surgery a couple hours ago."

"Surgery?" The words whispered past his lips as the images came flooding back to him. "Oh, God! Jed?!"

Lanai's eyes swelled, she began to nod, leaning in to hold her husband. She sobbed as the fear overwhelmed her emotions, her body bounced with each gasp of air.

20 minutes later an officer entered the room, he calmly sat Lanai down and stood by Rob's bedside. He explained the situation in its entirety. That Rob and Jed were mugged by someone they have in custody, some lowlife looking to steal the Mustang for some drug money. That Rob was shot once in the shoulder, he fell backward and lost consciousness, the bullet lodged into his shoulder blade. The officer's tone shifted as he began to talk about Jed, his eyes lowered and he looked to the ground. Jed was shot once, in the back of the head. He was pronounced dead by the first responders.

This didn't feel real. This was a dream, a horrible nightmare that Rob had originally assumed. His son was there, in front of him. Close enough he could have reached out and hugged him. If only another moment had passed, he would have. How could he have had everything back just to lose it in a blink of an eye? It wasn't fair. It wasn't supposed to happen this way!

Rob tried to get up, but the nurse stopped him. He winced in pain as his shoulder fired lightning quick responses to his nerves.

A couple of days passed as Rob stayed in the hospital. A handful of specialists came in and explained to him the recovery process, that he would need to rest his shoulder for a couple weeks and then he would need to start physical training at home. Not much was said in the last few days in the hospital, eventually, Lanai asked Rob about his thoughts on the funeral. What they should do? Where it should be held? There was a lot of planning to do and they needed to get on it. She was clearly stronger than Rob remembered. He recalled her being a mess the last time Jed died. Maybe it was because Jed was still a teenager? Maybe it was because he had lived more of his life and she didn't feel he was cut down in his prime?

Rob knew that wasn't it.

He knew why she was stronger this time around.

One of them had to be, and this time it was her. Last time, Rob was the one making the plans. Tending to her needs as she laid in bed for days on end. He was the one that called the funeral home. Called the flower shop. Called friends and family. He made the obituary, the playlist for the funeral, picked the final suit his young son would sleep in.

This time, it was Lanai. Rob's brain was switched off, he wasn't any help. Lanai assumed it was because of the traumatic experience and he was handling the best he could. She didn't have someone doing the heavy lifting, so as a strong woman, she had to do the lifting herself.

She wasn't wrong though, not entirely. Rob did switch his brain off. He felt like he failed his son. Rob did the worst possible thing to bring his son back, and selfishly, it backfired. Poor Marla's soul would forever rot in hell, in exchange for a handful of words with his son.

By the time Rob and Lanai left the hospital, everything for Jeds funeral was already arranged.

Lanai drove him outside Jed's apartment, where he had parked his car. They sat motionless for a moment as Rob stared into the parking lot. Imagining Jed waving as he walked down the stairs. Yelling at him as he strolled towards him. He didn't even see the man that would eventually kill his son. It all happened too fast and Rob was focused on only one thing.

"We are going to be okay," Lanai mumbled as she reached for his hand.

The sudden action startled Rob, snapping him back to life, "Yeah, I know." He reached back out for her hand, but she had already retracted it.

"We still have each other. We can do this," she reassured.

Rob patted her hand and kissed her cheek, "Everything will be better in the morning."

He exited the vehicle and waved goodbye.

Rob drove his car through the streets, unsure of where he was actually heading. He drove down neighborhoods after neighborhoods until he found a little park across town.

It was barely a park, if it wasn't for the old basketball court and the dilapidated swing set and slide, you would just think it was any other abandoned lot.

Rob parked his car in the first of only 5 parking spaces available. On the opposite end of the park, a man sat alone with a backpack.

He waited, watching the man do absolutely nothing.

A couple minutes turned into a handful of minutes; a handful of minutes turned into an hour. He sat in his car and watched the man the entire time.

The man must have noticed him, Rob wasn't positive when it happened. He stood up and meandered across the park. He was thin, unhealthily thin, his white tank top sagged down past the crotch of his pants. His pants were long and heavy, they swooped low and the man used one hand to hold them up as he walked. He had a black backpack strapped around one of his shoulders.

Rob didn't turn away as he finally approached his window, knocking with his knuckle extended.

He waited. Taking a couple quick breaths and exhaling, pressing the button down for the window to open.

"Can I help you?" The man said, his words were cold and didn't entirely feel like a question.

Rob thought about it for a moment, "What do you have?"

The man looked at Rob, his eyes squinted in disbelief, "Man, fuck you, get outta here."

He walked away from Rob.

Relief rolled over Rob, he snapped the car to life and pulled it into reverse. The car attempted to move backward before Rob slammed his foot on the brakes, pulling back into the parking spot and putting it in park.

The man was halfway back to his bench, creeped through the park.

Rob opened the door and followed the man.

Eventually, the man found his bench again, he sat down to see Rob approaching him.

"Hey, I told you to buzz off, bitch!" He said.

"Sorry," Rob said. "I haven't done this before, not on purpose anyway. I was nervous."

The man seemed unsure, he pulled the backpack off his back and placed it beside him on the bench.

"Seriously, man," Rob said. "Sorry about all that."

He unzipped the bag, pulling out a ziplock bag of a crystal substance that Rob assumed was Meth. "What are you looking for, chief?"

Rob didn't say anything.

The man placed the bag on his lap and reached into the backpack, "This shit I just got. Don't know much about it, but it'll fuck you up I hear." He pulled out another ziplock bag, the crystal was bright pink.

"That will do just fine," Rob said.

"Yeah?" The man gave a half smile, "Just fine?"

"Yeah, just fine."

"Ok," the man nodded his head. "That'll run ya 2-"

The words barely left his lips before Rob threw his gigantic fist into his face. Launching him over the bench, feet flying through the air. He tried to get up, but Rob was three times his size, he held him down with ease.

The skinny man tried to push Rob off, soon realizing it was in vain, tried to reach for his waistline. Rob pulled his arm back, forgetting he had a healing bullet wound in his shoulder. The second of hesitation allowed the man to reach a pistol which he tried to swing to Rob's face. Rob grabbed the man by the wrist, fighting through the pain in his shoulder. The man landed a solid punch to Rob's jaw.

Rob fell back, being sure to not lose his grip on the man's wrist.

Rob crawled back on top of the man, throwing punch after punch until the man dropped the gun and tried to shield his face.

To his right, Rob spied a softball sized rock in the ground. Using his free hand, he dug the rock out, cupped it in his hand, and swung it to the man's temple.

The rock made a deafening THUD as it connected.

The man's jaw stretched out; he whizzed a sharpening breath from his lungs. Rob swung again as a huge tear ripped at his hairline. The man's eyes rolled to the back of his head, his body twitched. He hurled the rock again, connected with the mouth, the teeth shattered in an instant, either flying from his mouth or clinging to the man's gums like a cliffhanger dangling from the edge. Blood drained from his wound as Rob threw the rock down over and over again until he was exhausted of life.

Rob tried to catch his breath. His heart was beating as fast as it had the previous night. He moved his hand over the man's face and rubbed as much blood as he could, placing it on the ground where he dug the rock out of.

"Blood for blood..." he began.

CHAPTER TWELVE

Rob opened his eyes to a new day.

He sat up and looked around the room, Lanai was asleep to his side. He patted her on the back and kissed her bare shoulder.

After Rob killed the man at the park, he drove home and was asleep by 6. Lanai seemed upset, there was much to do regarding Jed's funeral, but Rob knew it wouldn't matter. As soon as he opened his eyes, nothing from the last couple of days would have happened.

Rob stretched, long and hard. He reached into the closet and grabbed his robe, slipping it on as he moved towards the bathroom. Rob ran his hand over his bald dome, brushed his teeth and shaved.

He left the bathroom and pulled out his phone, dialing Jed's number.

The phone rang, only momentarily, before it went to voicemail.

Rob rang again, ending with the same result.

Now entering the kitchen, Rob passed the fridge while dialing once more. As the phone went to voicemail, he noticed on the fridge was a calendar.

That's one thing he missed about Lanai: the girl was organized. Even when life moved on, Jed moved out, she still mapped out each day as if they were still crazy as all hell. Instead of BASKETBALL PRACTICE or ORTHODONTIST APPT the days read such things as DATE NIGHT or OUR TIME.

Rob put his finger on the date, January 29th, in red marker it read: JED.

Rob remembered the phone call from earlier in the week, Jed was planning on spending the weekend home.

Possibly with his new girlfriend.

Rob opened his phone again, going to the text messages. He clicked on the conversation with Jed, revealing days' worth of conversations he had no memory of. He pressed the search button and typed in: Saturday.

The message jumped to the most recent line, Rob asking Jed if they should be expecting anyone else?

"He is bringing her," Rob smiled.

The idea was crazy. He had never put too much thought into the idea that Jed would have continued life, eventually meeting a partner.

But now, now that it was in front of him, it made him proud. He wanted to meet this young woman that swooped his son from him. The person who made Jed laugh and smile, brought him love and companionship. This woman was important to Jed, so by association, she was important to him too. He wanted to dive into the missing couple years of his son's life, and this would give him a perfect opportunity.

They could all sit around the dinner table and Rob could casually bring up random questions for Jed, playing it off for his girlfriends benefit, but ultimately not making it odd that his own father couldn't remember any events of his son's life for the last 5 years.

It was perfect.

"What's got you so smiley this morning?" Lanai asked as she strolled into the kitchen, planting a kiss on Rob's cheek.

"Nothing, just excited for dinner tonight," he said.

"You don't say?" She smiled back at him as she started the coffee pot.

Rob dug through the bowl of fruit, pulling out an apple, shining it on his robe, "I'm having a hard time remembering this girls name. What is it again?"

"Who? Anna?" Lanai said.

"Jed's girl?"

"Yeah, Anna."

"I'll try to remember that," he said. Rob took a bite of the apple, "I've tried to call him a couple times, went straight to voicemail."

"Already?" Lanai laughed, "It's literally 8 in the morning, give the kid some space, he'll be here soon enough."

Rob couldn't explain to her why he couldn't do that.

He shrugged and brought the apple to his mouth, he bit down his teeth felt like they splintered in his mouth. The apple was as hard as a rock.

Rob brought a hand to his mouth, he pulled his hand back to reveal a handful of blood, a white tooth fell to the ground.

"What the fuck?!" Rob screamed as he sprayed blood and teeth from his face. Blood painted the kitchen counter like a dying can of spray paint, it oozed off the counter and dropped to the floor.

He looked down at the apple, it was gone. Instead, cupped in his hand was a softball-sized rock, covered in blood.

"Rob?!" Lanai screamed.

Rob looked up at his wife, she looked confused.

"You okay? Did you hear anything I said?"

He looked down at his hand, the apple was back, his opposite hand was blood free. "Yeah, sorry, I was somewhere else."

"You look like it," she walked up and put the back of her hand on his forehead. "You sure you're up to tonight?"

Rob brushed her aside, "I'm fine. Promise."

Lanai gave a fake smile and walked back to the coffee pot, pouring into a matching his/her set of mugs.

"Hey, I was thinking maybe we'd see if Dave wanted to meet up for lunch?"

Lanai chuckled, handing Rob his mug, "Oh, you are serious?"

Grabbing the hot coffee, "Yeah? Why?"

"Mainly because you guys haven't talked for over 3 years," she said before blowing into her coffee. "Plus, the man's an asshole."

Rob sent a text to Jed, asking him to give him a call before he left town. He was hopeful he would get the message before he lost service. He was desperate to hear his voice again.

After a long shower and getting ready for the day, he thought back to what Lanai said in the kitchen. It made sense. The mystery to why he didn't have David's number in his phone was solved. Rob wanted to reach out to him, but that might not be an option until after Jed left this weekend.

What could have driven them apart? It's strange that in this healthier timeline, one where Rob wasn't a raging alcoholic, that their friendship wouldn't last? What could have happened that caused such a rift? He thought about asking Lanai, but there was no way to phrase the question without sparking questions from her.

Rob looked at his phone, half past 8. "Honey, what time is Jed getting in?"

No answer.

Rob stood up and yelled again.

Still nothing.

From the corner of his eye, he saw movement down the hall.

Rob followed the movement, against his better judgment. Inside his head he screamed as he crept closer to the front entrance to the house.

He briefly saw movement up the stairs, disappearing right beyond his visual reach. He took a small step towards the staircase, stopping just at the base.

CRASH!

A shattering of glass flew through the air, pelting him in the face. He looked down to see a fine layer of glass spread across the floor. The glass was thick and in small pebble sized chunks. The ground looked like a scene of a car crash once the cars were towed away. The lights in the hallway began to flicker, first leisurely before picking up pace. Soon it was as sudden as a strobe light.

It was her.

Marla.

Blood started to ooze off the top of the staircase. It slumped over to the next step, more blood flooding out to the next. It began to rush, soon it looked as if they had a dam upstairs that had broken free. Dark, rich blood began to flow from the steps, slamming against the wall and racing towards the floor.

"Nope," Rob said.

He grabbed his keys and exited the house.

Rob dialed his son's phone again; it rang and went to voicemail.

He sat at a booth at his favorite diner, some place he had gone as a child and rarely visited as an adult.

Or maybe not? He had no way of knowing if he had become a regular in the last 5 years.

Lanai had called while he was leaving the house, asking where he was going. He told her he needed to get some things for dinner and asked her what time they were expecting Jed. She said he would be in town no later than 3.

That meant he had over 6 hours to kill.

Rob ordered a chicken fried steak and a cup of black coffee. The waitress smiled and left. She didn't seem like she recognized him. He once again believed he wasn't a regular in this timeline either.

Opening his phone, he paused at the internet icon. He knew what he wanted to do, but he was hesitant. Rob hovered his finger above the phone for a full minute before pressing the icon, bringing to life the home screen to google.

Rob typed in: Marla. He stopped, trying as hard as he could to remember her last name.

He deleted her name and instead typed in: Group Grief Counseling Linkville.

The first result was the one he desired, he clicked the link and up popped the local group. He scrolled to the contact information, writing the number on a paper napkin. Rob moved his finger to the exit button before something caught his attention.

At the bottom of the menu a button that read: In Memory.

He clicked it.

The page opened, centered was a picture of Marla. She was a lot younger than Rob remembered her. Her blonde hair was curled around her shoulders, her smile was wide, her teeth bright white. Rob read the paragraph below her picture:

"In memory of our dear, Marla Everson. She was taken from us all too soon on the evening of July 18th, 2013. She was a beloved member of the group, recently graduating college from the University of Oregon with a degree in psychology and counseling, she moved to Linkville to open her own practice. Marla joined us January 20th and helped so many people in her short time with us. We will always remember her for her kind heart and her desire to help the community. Rest in Peace."

Rob read and reread the paragraph several times. Each time he hated himself more and more.

Rob milked the time he spent at the diner; he didn't have a lot of other things he could do. After about an hour he paid his check and left.

He dialed Jed again, still no luck.

The first snowflake hit Rob on the face, he looked up and watched little snowflakes fall from the sky like parachuting soldiers.

Rob checked his weather app on his phone, there weren't any big surprise snow storms rolling in. The forecast called for mild snow but it would be cleared up before noon. He double checked the pass to see if it would get dangerous for Jed, he was pleased to see that it was a clear day.

Little flakes peppered his windshield, he brushed them with the wipers. Rob made his way to the grocery store and followed through with what he had told Lanai. He grabbed some decent steaks, some fresh veggies, and some chips. Rob moved towards the cashier, passing the small corner of assorted flowers. Sunflowers, they were Becca's favorite.

Rob thought about picking some up for Lanai.

Something was off.

He wanted to grab them, he would of 5 years ago. What had changed? Lanai still acted the same way towards him, she was still adorable and loving. She still cared.

On the other hand, Rob had not lived the same couple of years as she had. The last 5 years saw the death of their son, the numbing breakup of their marriage, and the ugly side of a person that comes with the latter. He didn't blame her; he had done some horrible things throughout the entire thing. She had every right to leave, he would have judged her if she hadn't. He turned to the one thing that killed their son, he was a full-blown alcoholic within the first year.

That didn't change the fact that Rob had lived that life. Even though they seemed to be happy, Rob couldn't shake the feeling that things weren't. Rob still remembered that gut-wrenching feeling of discovering that Lanai had a new boyfriend. He remembered when David told him he heard they were engaged. He remembered the phone call he made to confirm it. Rob still had hope until that moment they could turn it all around and find their way back together. However, they never did. She remarried, and he got the once a year checkup.

His mind drifted to Becca.

He instantly felt shame that he hadn't thought of her once in the last week. Rob found himself down this road simply because he wanted David's help. He wanted to find a way to fix himself and live happily with Becca.

And at the end of the day, that road drove him in the opposite direction of her.

In this timeline, they most likely have never met.

Rob moved past the flowers and paid for his groceries.

A quarter to noon, Rob pulled into his house. He grabbed his bags and approached the house.

He was unsure of what would happen as he opened the door; he twisted the doorknob and pushed the door forward.

"Hey, honey!" Lanai said as walked down the stairs.

She extended her hands for the groceries, Rob handed them over and followed her to the kitchen.

"That took longer than I expected?" She said.

"Sorry, kinda got side-tracked. What have you been up to?"

"Just getting ready for tonight. Cleaning mainly."

The couple put the groceries away, continuing their small talk the entire time.

After the groceries were put away, the two of them sat down at the kitchen table.

Rob opened his phone and thought about calling Jed again, but decided better of it. Lanai was bound to get suspicious if he continued to call so frequently.

"I was thinking about what you said earlier," Lanai started.

"Yeah, what's that?"

"How we should reach out to David?"

Rob perked up, putting the phone face down, "What about it?"

"Maybe we should? You know, if you are ready to move on from the entire thing, why not try?"

Rob hoped that conversation would answer some of his questions. Instead, it only had him wondering more.

He needed answers.

"You know if I'm being honest..." Rob said, "I'm not even positive how it all went down anymore?" He gave a small chuckle.

"Yeah right!" She smiled, stretching out her arm to grab his empty hand. "It's really mature of you to make the first move."

"That's me," Rob said. "Mr. Fucking-Mature."

Lanai smiled, "No, seriously. I'm proud of yo-"

Her phone went off, the ringer a small background noise interrupting the conversation. She stood up and walked towards her purse on the kitchen counter.

"I'm proud of you. I'm not going to lie, I am surprised that you brought all this up. It's been over a year since we've even talked about him." Lanai dug her phone from her purse.

"Oh, it's Anna," she said.

"Jed's Anna? You have her number?"

She nodded as she answered.

"That would have been helpful earlier," Rob muttered under his breath.

"Wait. Wait. Calm down," Lanai said, her voice got higher, shakier. "I don't understand."

Rob jumped from the chair, leaping to Lanai as she brought her hand to her mouth.

"No!" She screamed as she dropped the phone.

Rob sat quietly on the ground of the kitchen floor, holding his wife in both arms.

After Lanai dropped the phone Rob picked it up, an officer that reported to the scene was just getting on the opposite end, he said Anna was having a hard time and asked if it would be okay if he brought them up to speed.

Jed and Anna had pulled over at a rest stop on their way into town, both of them wanted to stretch their legs so they went for a short walk around the river that neighbored the rest stop. They strolled down a small path that cut through trees and was bordered by white snow on each side. Jed suggested they cross the river on the south side at a long metal bridge, the trail would follow the river back towards another metal bridge on the north side, they could follow that trail back to the car and get back on the road.

According to Anna, Jed was having fun and joking around. He wanted to try and walk on the railing of the bridge, asking Anna to hold his hand for balance. She said she wouldn't do it, but Jed eventually pressured her into it. Jed galloped on top of the rail with ease, even turning around and walking backward at the end of the bridge. They followed the trail back north to the next bridge, where he confidently climbed back on the rail, this time not asking for Anna's help.

At the midpoint of the bridge it began to hide below the shadows of a giant pine tree, Anna said Jed didn't notice the ice that had still clung to the cold metal. His foot made contact with the ice and his foot slid out from under him. She reached out to grab him, but it was too late. He dropped into the water back first, Anna said she waited for him to pop back up, but after what felt like forever, she began to panic. She jumped into the icy river after him, landing close to where she watched him disappear. Anna claimed she immediately found him, he looked terrified as he panicked to get his foot loose from the river floor. They fought and fought to release him, but the current was too strong and Anna couldn't help as she was flushed away with the river. She sprinted back to the car and called 9-1-1.

That was over an hour ago.

About the time that Rob stood staring at a display of flowers, thinking about someone else.

While he was standing there thinking about his old life, Jed was fighting for his and lost.

A knot grew in his stomach, Rob stood up and dry heaved into the sink.

He ran the sink and took a long drink from the running water.

Rob looked down at Lanai, who was crying into her hands. He thought about going over and comforting her, the way he had done the first time Jed died. But that was five years ago and he felt the relationship had changed a lot in the last five years ago. He couldn't put a finger on it, but something felt *off* about Lanai. Would Jed feel *off* if he ever saw him again? Would it live up to everything he dreamed it would be? There was only way he would find out.

Pushing the water off, Rob moved away from the sink and stepped over Lanai as he walked out of the kitchen.

"Where are you going?" Lanai asked.

Rob didn't answer as he threw a coat on and reached for his keys.

She won't remember anything anyhow.

He needed to find someone worthy of dying. No matter what, he was going to see his son again.

CHAPTER THIRTEEN

18 months later.

Rob gathered his breath as he approached the front steps to a nice, suburban house. The front yard was meticulously maintained. The edge walkway was highlighted with an array of beautiful flowers that gave a splash to color to the rich green of the yard. In the center of the yard was a decent sized tree, the leaves were a dark purple, white blossoming flowers spread throughout the tree like a wildfire.

Finally, at the doorway, Rob raised his fist to the door before deferring to ring the doorbell. He heard the jingle ring through the inside of the house. Rob rehearsed his opening line to himself under his breath. It was only 4 words, but if he didn't concentrate, he would surely mess it up.

The door opened; David's smile disappeared as his eyes met Rob's.

Nothing. Neither man said anything for what felt like an eternity. With each passing moment, Rob felt the tension building like a volcano about to explode.

"I don't think so," David said as he turned from the door.

Rob pushed his hand out, blocking the door from closing, "We need to talk."

"No," David asserted, "we don't."

Rob towered over David, his gigantic stature rising over David, not unlike the biblical David and Goliath. He pushed the door harder, opening it wider and sliding David out of the way. "I really don't give two fucks that we don't talk anymore. I need your help."

As the words left his mouth, his eyes locked onto the small boy standing beside David. Rob felt like a prick, he didn't want to overpower David in front of his son. He didn't want to be responsible for deflating the kid's image of his father.

David took notice too, asking his son to go outside with his brother. The kid looked from his father to Rob and back to his father, unsure of the situation. “Now,” David’s tone growled; the kid sprinted away.

“We have nothing to talk about, Robbie,” David said struggling behind the door. “Get off my property!” He heaved the door with all of his strength, almost closing the door before Rob dropped his large boot in between it.

“Blood for blood. Life for a life,” Rob said.

David’s face froze, he stopped pushing the door but didn’t release it either. “Where did you hear that?”

“You told me.”

“No, I would remember that.”

Rob gave a gentle push, David didn’t fight him, “Why do you think that is?”

They exchanged few words as Rob entered the house. David led the way to the living room, pointing to the couch for Rob to take a seat. He left to the kitchen, before returning with a beer in both hands, he hesitantly tossed one to Rob.

Rob nodded his head in exchange for a *Thank you.*

With the beers opened, Rob began to talk. He explained the abridged version, telling him about the accident that took Jed's life. He told them about the night David brought him to the park and explained how it worked. That David killed a man from Minnesota. How he wasn't able to get to Jed in time, not being able to get to him before he was murdered.

"Can you prove any of this?" David asked.

"What do you mean?"

"How do I know that all of this is true? I don't know how you know about the man from Minnesota, maybe I told you all this years ago when I was shit-faced? Maybe you decided you needed to come here and make me look like a fool for your own pleasure?"

"Maybe? To be honest I have no idea why we are fighting? I woke up and my entire life had fast-forwarded to a point I know nothing about. I lost a lot of things when I opened my eyes that morning, one of them was my best friend."

David didn't say anything.

"I can't prove it to you, because as you understand, that version of you is gone. That life I had, is gone. I know that more than likely you still have a folded obituary in your wallet, I don't know why that would change?"

As if that was all the proof David needed, his brows squinted, and he nodded. "Okay, so if I did tell you all of this and you went through with it... it would restart from the moment Jed died. You would wake up and the entire world would have continued. I guess I could believe that. We haven't talked for over 2 years, so it was at least that long ago. When was it?"

Rob took a long sip from his can, "6 years ago tomorrow."

"Holy hell!" David yelled. "You reset 6 years?"

"No," Rob admitted, "I reset 5."

David scratched the top of his head, "What?"

"You told me all of this a year and a half ago, at least."

"But you said that you haven't actually had any time with Jed yet? How have you not seen him? In the last year, he has been around for Christmas and New Years? I've seen him around town on various weekends? Help me understand?"

"Every time I reset the timeline; he dies before I get to him. It doesn't matter if he is in front of me before I can even give him a hug, he dies. If he is back in college, he might live longer, a couple weeks so far is the longest. Eventually though, he dies."

David put his hand out as if he was trying to get the attention of an out-of-control driver, "Wait. Wait, how many times have you reset the timeline?"

Rob gritted his teeth, holding back the tears that felt like his eyes were a dam about to collapse. "48 times."

"48 times?!" David stood up and began to pace around the living room. "48 times?"

"At least."

"You've killed 48 people?" David asked, his hands pressed against his head.

"At least that many."

"Why? I don't know what I told you, but I would have at least told you to expect that. That it wasn't a permanent solution. Jed was already dead. His number would sooner or later be drawn again."

"I know," Rob dipped his head ashamed.

"Then why?"

"Because I gave up everything to have Jed back. Everything. My life finally started making sense. I had a beautiful girl; we had a life together! For the first time in years, I was getting back into graphic design! I didn't want to lose all that if I can't even give my own son one last hug. One last kiss on his forehead. One last *I love you*. You got all of that with your wife. I haven't even gotten a sip."

David sighed. Rob could see he didn't agree with his actions, but he could tell that he could understand it at the very least.

"Listen, I can't really explain it. At first, it was a mistake or something along those lines. Almost every single person that I killed I regret. It has served no purpose and I've caused so much pain. Pain that I understand. Pain that no one should have to go through. I hate myself every time, maybe not immediately, but there comes a point each time where I feel like I'm a monster. But now I'm at 48, and I can't go on. I need this to stop."

"Then stop."

"I can't yet."

A wave of silence flushed over the men, Rob dried his eyes and leaned back into his chair.

"What do you need my help with?" David said.

"I want to talk to Penny's uncle."

The drive was awkward.

David asked a neighbor to watch the boys so they could make the trip alone. Rob sat in the passenger seat of David's large pickup. The pickup that Rob always thought David had lifted an extra six inches to compensate for his lack of height.

After a couple blocks, Rob broke the silence, "You didn't tell me they would try to kill me."

"Who?"

"The poor souls I've damned."

"I can't vouch for that version of me, but I'm sure I would have said something. It never goes away, kind of an important thing to know. And they shouldn't be trying to *kill* you, just make your life a living hell."

"It never goes away?" Rob fixated on that part.

"Not yet anyway. Think about it. What would happen to them if they did manage to kill you?"

Rob thought about it, "If I died? I guess they'd go too."

"Exactly, and where is the next stop for them?"

"Hell," Rob said. He felt his heart drop as once again the guilt ate at him like a rat trying to eat its way out of his chest.

"As long as you are alive, they aren't spending literally in hell. Figuratively, yes. Being stuck with you would seem like a nightmare. But it's in their best interest to keep you alive for as long as possible."

"So, you've had that kid from Minnesota terrorize you since then?"

"Yeah, I find it hard to believe I didn't tell you it would happen?" David asked.

"Well, ya didn't."

"I'm sorry. I should have told you. It haunts me every night," David said.

"What was that?"

"What? It haunts me every night?" David repeated.

"Shit," Rob said to himself. "Shit. You did tell me. I just didn't know you literally meant you were haunted every night?"

"Well, that's what happens."

"David," Rob said, "if you ever decide to tell someone else... you need to make yourself clearer here. Food for thought."

"I guess I do," David chuckled. "My bad."

The men sat quietly as the pickup hummed down a neighborhood not far from Rob's own house.

"48 people haunt you? How often does it happen?" David asked.

Rob looked down at his blood-soaked hands, behind his hands the floorboard was covered in a thick layer of blood. It clung to his shoes and pants, oozing from the dash like syrup. "At this point, it's damn near constant."

"Shit, man."

"Yeah, shit."

A moment passed as Rob closed his eyes, hoping the horror in front of him would pass. It was something that he had picked up after his first dozen experiences. Sometimes if he ignored it, closing his eyes would push it away momentarily.

He opened his eyes to see a tall dark-skinned man sitting in between David and himself. His neck had a gash that would fit a broken beer bottle into because when Rob had met him he had shoved just that into the man's throat. He recognized the man as victim 27. Michael Underwood.

"What happens when you reset the timeline again? You wake up tomorrow and I don't remember any of this? Are you going to hunt me down and try to convince me again?"

"That's not going to be a problem," Rob said as he tried to not pay attention to the bleeding man beside him. That man spit blood onto the windshield.

"Why's that?"

"Because I reset it last night. As far as I'm aware Jed is alive, he has been having a hard since his fiancée died back about six months ago. I imagine he is just trying to make it through the day."

"Wait... did you kill someone last night?" David mumbled.

Rob didn't answer, he turned and looked out the window as houses flew by.

Outside the window of the car, the street was dotted with blood-soaked people, both men, and women. Some older than Rob, some as much as ten years younger. Each one wore their violent deaths like a badge of honor. Blood dripping from various limbs and holes in their bodies. Dent heads and slit throats.

The old man was waiting for them to arrive, David had called and asked if he was available to talk, the old man didn't hesitate in the slightest. He introduced himself as Ben and shook Rob's hand with a grip that was unexpected. Ben welcomed them in, ushering them to the back patio where he had iced tea and crackers waiting on a glass table.

"Help yourself," he said.

"Thanks, Ben," Rob said, "but I'll have to pass."

Ben looked to David who was already picking at the crackers.

"Sit, sit," he patted a cushioned chair. "What brings you here?"

"I would like to ask you some questions?" Rob said.

"About the curse," Ben said as he poured some tea from the pitcher into a small glass.

"Yeah, how did you know?" David said as he pulled a chair next to Rob and said down.

"Because, David, I don't think you and I have ever talked about anything other than that?" He said with a wry smile.

Rob looked at David, "I guess that's true," David said.

"I'm guessing one of two things have happened..." Ben started, "either you, Rob, have lost someone recently and David said he knows a way to bring them back and you came to me, or David stupidly decided he needed to tell you himself and it's already happened."

David ducked his head.

"I'm guessing it's the latter."

Ben took a drink from his tea, he sat down in a chair across the glass table and looked out over his backyard. "Have you already done it or are you planning on doing it?"

"I've already done it," Rob admitted.

The old man nodded his head, "I see."

"How do you remember talking to David about it? If you really talked to him after Penny's death, the first time, you shouldn't be able to remember it?"

Ben turned around, pulling a rolled cigarette from the pocket of his shirt. He gave it a small lick and stuck it in his mouth, he pulled a single match from the same pocket and with a flick of his fingers it ignited. He puffed the cigarette a couple of times until it was good to go, "By watching David at the funeral. I remember as he buried his wife how composed he was. Never had I talked to the man until that day and when I came up to give my condolences, he thanked me before I even got to him. I put it together from there. Is that why you came here?" He shook his head, "No, no you have a larger question."

"How do I make it stick?"

"You can't," David answered. "I told you, dead is dead. It'll one day catch up to him."

Rob ignored his friend, "How do I bring him back, for good?"

Ben inhaled the cigarette and looked across the table at Rob as if he was seeing into his very existence. He looked through his eyes and saw what he wanted, a man that truly would do anything to reach his goal. "There is a way, I have been told."

Both men froze, waiting for the old man to continue.

"It was your son, wasn't it?"

Rob nodded his head.

"The curse calls for a life for a life, and by damning someone else to hell, the curse gives you more time with your son. This isn't something to be taken lightly, you are literally taking an innocent person and damning them to eternal damnation. The trick to having it stick is the same, but with a twist."

"What is that?"

"You have to find someone willing to trade places with your son. Somebody has to be willing to trade in their own life for your sons."

Rob thought about it for a moment, "How do I do that?"

"I don't know. To be perfectly honest, I'm not positive it actually works."

The man took a final drag from his cigarette and exhaled.

CHAPTER FOURTEEN

"I'm not helping you, Rob," David asserted.

"It's the only way," Rob said.

"No, it is time to let go. For Christ's sake, you've been down a similar road over 48 times. It's time to move on."

"I can't, I've come so far, broken everything over and over. I have to finish this."

"Well, I won't take any part of it."

"So, if I killed myself, right now, and you'll just let that be it."

"Yes, and seeing how we are here, in my house, I'd prefer it if you didn't please."

"Maybe I'll talk to Lanai?"

"She won't believe you."

Rob dropped his head; he knew David was right. He needed someone with him, someone had to put his blood to the earth and someone had to say the words. Rob could feel it, deep within himself, he was so close. The answer was here, he just wasn't able to find it yet. Somehow this would have to work.

"How are you and Lanai doing, by the way?" David asked.

"I don't know, man. It's hard."

David bobbed his head, "I can see that. You've literally been living moment to moment for the last year and a half, no wonder you're bald." He smiled.

"Believe it or not, I think this was by choice?" He said pointing to his bald head. "It's just that, everything feels different now. This was everything I wanted so long ago, to have my family back and my life back. But now that I spent so long not having it, it doesn't feel real. It feels artificial. As if I am the only person who knows how things are supposed to be. Lanai is supposed to be happily married to that douchebag doctor-guy. She doesn't even know about it. When she kisses me, it feels like there is no spark from my end. If it wasn't for me resetting everything every couple of days, I'm sure she would have caught on by now. I don't know what's changed... but something's different."

David lowered his head, "I know what changed."

Rob thought about it for a moment, staring at his only friend through squinted eyes, suddenly it made sense. "That's it. Why we haven't talked for years. That's why Lanai was so shocked when I was going to invite you over."

"Rob, I'm so sorry. Honestly, it was a mistake, it just happened one night and I wish I could take it back, but I can't."

Rob throw his hand and the air and waved, "I don't know why, but I'm not even upset."

"You're not?"

"I mean, that happened to a different me. Someone that isn't here now, I know it was me but it was *wasn't me*. I'm honestly not surprised. It all makes sense."

Rob's mind shifted gears, Becca came into focus.

A couple of months ago he was desperate enough he reached out to her. She had taken the job in Clover Cove as he always assumed she would. It brought him back to the night he left her at their house when she denied turning down her dream job to be with him. If she never met him, she would have gone after all. He drove up to Clover Cove one day in April, waiting in the staff parking lot until he saw her leave the hospital. His heart was flooded with all kinds of emotions. He wanted to race up to her and hold her. Kiss her. Smell her. Love her. He had been away from her for over a year, but the moment he saw her again all those emotions raced back to him. Rob didn't move, he watched her get into her car and drive off.

She was no different than Jed. No matter how much he wanted to get to her, he couldn't. She wouldn't remember him. As far as she was concerned, he doesn't exist.

Rob's phone buzzed in his pocket, he pulled it out and stared at it.

"What? Who is it?"

Rob didn't answer, the phone finally stopped buzzing, and he continued to look at his phone like it was the craziest thing he has ever seen. The light bulbs in his head were warming up, the lights were beginning to turn on. The idea was forming.

"I've got it."

Rob's timing was perfect, as Lanai was out of the house running errands as she tended to do on a

Saturday afternoon. He went upstairs and went straight for the closet, reaching up to the top shelf and pulled out his pistol. Rob checked the clip; it was ready to go.

In and out of the house in no time flat, he pulled onto the street and headed north out of town.

There was one thing he wanted to do first.

The drive was long, just shy of 8 hours. He had made the trip numerous times, and each time he seemed more desperate than the last. Each time the trip seemed to take longer and longer.

Finally, he passed the welcoming sign of Clover Cove.

Rob pulled his car to the first real store he saw and parked. He ran inside, trying to gauge where in the store he needed to go, then took off again.

He found the random corner of the store that had a beautiful display of various flowers.

Rob probed through the display for a moment before he found what he was looking for. He pulled out a beautiful bouquet, a gorgeous yellow sunflower the center of attention.

Rob smiled at it, it made everything almost feel normal again.

He paid for the flowers and sprinted back to his car, staring at his watch as he moved.

Half an hour, he gathered. If she was working today, then he had about half an hour until her shift would end.

Rob pulled into the hospital's staff parking lot and in a short time spotted her car.

"Yes," he said to himself.

He pointed his car into the first empty spot and turned the car off.

Rob watched the exit of the hospital, soon enough she would be there. His heart began to race, it was exciting every time. Every time he saw her, he got butterflies

Hairs on the back of his neck stood straight up like an electrical current was surging through his body. He looked to the top of the windshield; blood began to drip from above. Sliding down the windshield, as thick as syrup. It obscured his vision. He couldn't see the door where any moment Becca would come out to her car.

"Not now, seriously. Not now," Rob pleaded.

He rolled his window down, sticking his head out so he could see clearly.

In the mirror, he caught a glimpse of someone.

He turned around as he saw a bloody woman walk towards him, victim 29. Rob remembered her with clarity. It was the closest he had ever gotten to Jed; he had grabbed his arm to pull him in for a hug and out of nowhere a car jumped a curb and plowed through him. He remembered rubbing Jed's blood from his face in horror as he raced to his side. The woman had gotten out to see what happened, she began to cry when she saw that Jed's body was practically torn in half. Rob held his son's hand as he whispered to him how much he loved him, watching as his son took his last breath (one of his many last breaths). As soon as his pulse was gone for good, Rob stood up and charged the woman.

It was the fastest he had ever killed someone and damned their soul to hell after Jed had died. It was the only time that Rob didn't feel overwhelming guilt as he uttered the last sentence of the curse.

She deserved it, he told himself.

Now she was once again pissing him off. Her face was swollen and bloodied the same way as it was that day. Curly brown hair matted in a thick red mass where her skull was caved in. Her jogging shirt and yoga pants were torn and bloodied. She had only one shoe on, Rob assumed it was because he had knocked her so hard that one of her foot flung the shoe off like a rocket.

Victim 29 lunged out for him, grabbing him around the neck. He could feel her wet hands clamp down, digging into his flesh as deep as she possibly could. Rob broke free and shoved her back, rolling the window up and blocking her out.

"Fuck off," he yelled.

"You're not going to get rid of her like that, you know?" Said a voice from behind him.

Rob didn't look into the mirror; he knew who it was. Victim 27.

The only one that didn't take it personally and talked to him.

It was too bad Rob couldn't stand the guy; he bugged the living shit out of him almost as much as he did when he was alive.

"You can fuck off too, Eric," Rob said as he turned on the wipers. The blood on the windshield smeared and streaked across the window, not doing much.

"That's not going to work," Eric said.

"I know that, Eric! Jesus, just shut up!"

Eric leaned in between the front seats, his head was a large hole in his head of exposed bone and brain. The left eye was completely white, the right eye was still a lively blue. His head still dripped the blood from his wound, onto his workout gear he had sported the day Rob killed him. "I'm just trying to help you, buddy."

"Then get rid of her, that would fucking help. Maybe you could finally do something productive."

"You know I can't control her."

Rob didn't answer, he looked down at his watch.

Any minute.

Any minute she would come out to her car.

"Eric, when I get back, you better be gone," he said, grabbing the flowers from the passenger seat and exiting the mustang.

Rob picked up his pace as victim 29 reached out for him, her fingers grazed his shoulder as he pulled past her. A few more steps and she was left completely behind him.

The door to the parking lot opened, out stepped Becca.

Rob slowed his pace; he didn't want to scare her off.

"Excuse me, miss?" He said as unalarming as he could.

Becca looked up from her phone, seeing Rob waving at her. She smiled at him.

The first time she'd smiled at him in a year and a half. His heart swelled with desire. He missed her, missed her smile. Rob could feel the need for her rise in his heart.

"Excuse me, I don't mean to bother you," he said.

"Not a problem," she said. "How can I help you?"

Rob held the flowers to his chest, "This is going to sound strange, but please bear with me."

Becca chuckled.

God, I missed that too, he thought.

"Um, so I was visiting a buddy here a couple days ago and saw you."

Becca's chuckle stopped, he was heading into a creepy territory and he needed to get out before it was too late.

"No, it's nothing like that. You looked just like my ex-fiancée, who died. Literally, you could be her twin. Her name was... Tess."

Her smile slowly crept back to life.

"I'm heading out of town, and I would never be able to live with myself if I didn't see you one more time. You are not her; I know that. You've had a completely different life. I know you don't know me and this is the strangest thing to ever happen to you. But, if you would be so kind, I bought you these," Rob held out the flowers.

Becca hesitantly took them, the smile finally formed, "Sunflowers are my favorite."

"Really?" Rob played it off, "They were hers too."

"Well, thank you, stranger," Becca said as she pulled out an envelope that had been tucked in with the flowers. "What's this?"

"Give it a read once you get home. I've got to get going, but seeing you right now was exactly what I needed. Have a wonderful life, young lady."

Becca laughed, "You too, stranger." She reached her arms out for a hug.

Becca was a hugger, but it still caught him by surprise as she wrapped her little arms around him. Rob held her back, only long enough that when she was ready to release, he did too. She smelled like lavender.

"Goodbye, kid."

CHAPTER FIFTEEN

Almost a full day had passed since he got the phone call while at David's house. The call was from Lanai, he didn't have to answer it to know what it was about.

Once again, Jed had died.

It was a weird feeling not knowing how it happened. With everything he had seen in the last 18 months, each time his son died it was somehow different. It was like the universe had an endless supply of ways to kill a person and it was just having fun with it.

Rob rolled into the Linkville Cemetery and parked in his usual spot across the street. He rolled his window down and opened a fresh pack of cigarettes, lighting one for the last time. Rob had planned it all out but was still nervous about what was to come next. The cigarette quivered in his fingers like a high school students' pencil taking their SATs.

Beside him at the passenger seat, was the pistol. He watched the pistol as he blew smoke from between his lips.

"Okay," he said to the weapon, "let's go."

Rob crossed the street, with the pistol in his pocket. Everything had to go just right, but he was positive it would. He finished off the cigarette and flicked the butt in the air as the first drop of rain slammed to the earth. Rob lowered his head as the rain picked up, the clouds rolled and the thunder rang out as it quickly became a storm. He pulled the hoodie of his sweatshirt over his head and continued to look down as he made his way around the cemetery to the tree, he used to hope the closed gate.

"Don't do it, Rob," a voice said.

Rob looked up to see the last person he wanted to see.

Eric, victim 27. The raindrops bounced off his ghostly body as if he was still alive. The water cascaded through the hole in his head, turning blood red as it seeped out.

"You don't know what you're doing," Eric insisted as Rob passed him.

"Eric, if all this does it gets rid of you, I've accomplished something."

Rob kept pace, moving around the edge of the cemetery as his sweatshirt began to become wholly soaked. Eric appeared again as he peeled around the corner.

"Go back, Eric."

"Back where?" Eric asked.

"I don't fucking know! Just, wherever the hell you come from when you aren't here!" Rob passed Eric again. He didn't follow, Eric turned around and watched Rob move towards the tree.

Rob climbed the tree the same way he had done it all the times before, he sprinted the last couple steps to the tree. His feet splashed in the freshly formed puddles of mud at the base of the tree. With ease, Rob grabbed the lowest branch and pulled his body up. Rob sat up on the branch, the tree was too large for the rain to penetrate. It was a nice relief to be dry momentarily.

He positioned himself and stood up on the thick branch and began to walk above the fence line.

CREAK!

Rob rolled his head towards the sound, buried in the darkness of the tree behind him. He waited to hear it again.

CREEAK!

He found the direction, it was behind him, but it was also the next branch above him. He looked up.

Blood dripped from the shadows, it landed on his hand and arms. Rob rubbed the blood on his soggy sweatshirt and watched the blood fall.

The darkness felt like a black hole, swallowing up any light that could possibly reach it and only giving back a black void.

A hand curled out from the branch, it was thin and pail. The nails were artificially pink, except the thumb which didn't exist anymore. It was just a deep pocket of blood.

Rob knew who it was, only one victim had fought back so hard that Rob was almost positive he would become the victim by the end of the night. Victim 13.

She pulled her head out of the shadows, her scalp was almost completely gone. He could see her bare bone, the white shined through the shadows with ease.

Her face was swollen and bruised; she had put up a hell of a fight. He could see the knife wound in her shoulder as she lowered further.

Rob took a step back, towards the cemetery.

In the blink of an eye, she lunged from the branch, reaching out like a rabid spider monkey. She hit Rob, who at nearly 300 lbs generally wouldn't have been affected by the small woman's weight, but while balancing on the branch, it was more than enough to send him toppling over.

Rob slammed to the earth shoulder first, he felt his shoulder pop as the pain shot through his nerves like a sprinter after hearing the shot of the pistol. He rolled over and tried to get up, but victim 13 crawled with him. On all fours, her ass pointing to the sky, she crawled with her head faced out to him.

Rob kicked out, connecting with her jaw. He kicked again and again until he felt his boot kick through her jaw. It dangled loosely from her face, like a chinstrap to a football helmet.

With a couple more kicks in her direction, he was free. He stood up and turned towards the cemetery. It wasn't as empty as he expected. In the dark of the night, he could make out shadows moving behind gravestones and markers. Behind the painfully manicured bushes and trimmed trees.

He didn't know how many people waited ahead of him, but he guessed it was in the ballpark of 48.

"They aren't ready to go," Eric said as he appeared to Rob's side. "Not yet."

"Why? They are already gone."

"Not completely. They might all hate you, but while you're alive, they aren't damned yet."

Rob looked at Eric for the first time in a while and didn't see victim 27. He saw the awkwardly tall ginger out for a morning jog at the wrong place at the wrong time. He still wore his short jogging pants and a zip-up hoodie. "I didn't know."

"Yeah. It's a pretty shit deal. We are damned to follow you around for as long as possible. We have to follow you and watch you every moment of your miserable life until you eventually die. Then once that's all done, we get to spend eternity being tortured in hell."

"How do you know this?" Rob said.

"I don't know," Eric scratched his face below his bloody hole. "We just do."

"Do you know if this is going to work?" Rob asked.

Eric shook his head, "No, but whether or not it does means only one thing for us. Our time is up. We've only got one more stop."

"I'm sorry, Eric."

Eric smiled somewhat, "I know you are. That's why I never took it personally."

"I should have been nicer to you."

Eric chuckled, "You were dealing with it the best you could. I was extra annoying on purpose."

"Can I ask you a question before I take off?" Rob said.

"Hit me with it," Eric said.

"All those nights you spent at the tavern, what brought you there?"

Eric seemed confused, in this timeline he never met Rob at the tavern, he was unaware they even had that history. He smiled, "life had a habit of kicking me around when I was alive. Long story short, it was a girl."

"Ex?" Rob asked.

Eric nodded his head, "yeah."

Rob smiled at him as he felt a finger at his ankle, he jumped forward and saw victim 13, she had managed to catch up with him.

"I've got to go," he said as he backed away from 13. "I'm sorry, Eric. Really, I am."

"Well, I hope it works out for you, Rob. Otherwise, it was all for nothing. Either way, I'll be seeing you," he waved as he turned around and walked away.

"See ya," Rob said to himself with a smile, before he realized where he would see Eric again. "Fuck."

Most of the victims would be no better off than victim 13, they wouldn't be able to keep up with him as he moved through the gravestones. There would be some that could still keep up with him, and even some that could outrun him. Those were the ones that Rob was most worried about. People that were at the peak performance of their life and felt robbed of watching their bodies decline naturally.

Rob had made this walk what felt like hundreds of times, he could get to the back right of the grounds with little effort, using the majority of his focus on the shadows and those that were trying to stop him.

He began to jog, his feet squishing into the wet grass at a solid rhythm as he zig and zagged away from the first couple of victims that only watched as he moved past.

Rob paused for a moment as he saw someone, he hadn't seen in what felt like forever. Victim 1. Marla had her back to him; she faced a gorgeous faux marble gravestone. Rob hesitated as he moved behind her to see that it was her own marker.

"You never had a chance to see it, did you?"

She nodded no.

"I'm sorry, Marla."

She didn't respond, none of them spoke unless it was Eric.

He reached out and placed his hand on her shoulder, she placed her own bloody hand on his.

After a few moments passed, he moved on. He picked his jog up to a sprint as he saw some of the angrier victims. They tried to keep up to with him, but they didn't know the cemetery grounds well enough to catch him before they even could come within arm's reach, Rob slipped away and was gone.

Rob moved shadow to shadow, zigging and zagging like he had done back in high school football, avoiding tacklers and even giving a good stiff-arm or two.

Another victim stopped Rob in his steps.

The girl didn't move after him, she never came after him. She only appeared to Rob when he was at his lowest. She would appear to him, the blood, the smell of her rotting body, the regret. Of all the people she killed, this was the one that truly haunted him.

Rob victim 24, Anna.

It wasn't planned out; she never did anything that truly upset Rob. She seemed sweet. Anna seemed to honestly care for Jed, in the way that Rob always hoped someone would. She just happened to be the person Rob blamed at that given moment, she was in range and Rob was blinded by rage.

"How could you let this happen, again?!" He could remember screaming at her as he strangled the life from her. Rob had convinced himself that she was the key to it. Seeing how she was always with him when he died, it didn't take much for Rob to convince himself.

Rob regretted it. It didn't change anything and he took away something from Jed that he could never give back. He proposed to her only a couple months before...

He wasn't able to move on, and neither was she.

She only cried as Rob passed her.

Rob wished he could take it back.

He wished he could take it all back.

Finally, Rob found what he was looking for.

Jed's plot.

They had bought the 3 plots years before Jed even died when he was 15, it was Lanai's idea. She rationalized that this way they all 3 could be together for forever. Over 50 times a hole has been dug and re-dug, a coffin (surprisingly not always the same kind) lowered over and over again. He wasn't at every funeral, sometimes it was too sudden or it was too difficult to go again, but he was at most.

Rob walked up to the plot; the hole already perfectly cut out of the earth. He looked inside to the emptiness inside, the dark hole that seemed to go on for miles.

A hand reached out of the hole, gripping the grass above and pulling itself out of the ground. His muscles pulled his blue jumpsuit tight as his large body stood straight. Rob rarely felt the sense of what he imagined a child felt looking up at an adult, but even for Rob's large size, this man towered in both height and weight. His jumpsuit stained with blood at his shoulders and chest, the blood still looked wet and tacky. His bald head had tattoos that were covered in a black bandana when Rob had first met him, over a year ago. This was one of the many victims that were a matter of convenience. It was also the one victim he wished he had known a little more about before he drove a shovel through his throat.

Cameron, victim 8. An ex-con, freshly released from jail. Landed a job as the groundskeeper at the cemetery. He was an angry man with an angrier past.

Rob wished that he hadn't walked up behind him as he was finishing up his day of work, grabbing the shovel from the back of his work truck and killing him as he left the cemetery that day.

He watched as the man came out of the hole, he stood up and smiled at Rob. The beast of a man sprinted towards Rob, who tried to absorb the impact as they both fell to the ground. He tried to push him off of him, but 8 just grabbed him by the shoulder. The action reminded Rob how his shoulder was no longer connected to his body.

8 head-butted Rob, connecting his forehead with Rob's nose. Blood exploded from his face; his eyes saw stars.

Rob reached into his jacket pocket and pulled out the pistol, bringing it to his head.

"Stop!" He yelled, "All I need to do is pull the trigger and you are fucking gone!"

8 smiled, "You won't. You still need to say that fucking bullshit to save your precious Jed."

He walked over to Rob and reached for the gun; Rob fired once at 8's chest.

The man fell back and reached for where his heart was. He removed his hand to reveal no damage. 8 stomped back to Rob and kicked the gun from his hand, it flew into the dark hole.

Rob watched the gun get swallowed by the darkness, he looked up to see a boot slam into his already broken nose. He felt bones in his cheek shatter as the man stomped another time.

His face was quickly becoming as grim as many his victims, at that moment Rob began to wonder if this was what every one of them felt in their final moments alive? The pain? The disbelief? The millions of things they still had to do; would they cross their mind? The loved ones they were leaving behind, would they worry about them?

Again, the boot came down, this time 8 fell over with a grunt.

Rob blinked a couple times, bringing his hands to his eyes and tried to brush the buildup of blood and rain from his sockets. He looked over and saw Eric grappling with the man that was easily triple his size.

The mountain of a man rolled Eric to his back and pinned him down. Eric kicked and tried to wiggle his way out, but it was useless. 8 placed both of his knees on Eric's shoulders, bringing his hands to Eric's face. He put both hands into Eric's giant hole in his face and put both fingers around the outside of the hole.

"No!" Eric squealed.

Rob tried to raise himself, but finding balance wasn't as easy. He turned around and saw that another broken victim grabbing at him.

8 pulled both hands away from each other, expanding the hole until his face ripped clean in halves. It sounded like a water balloon popping on the ground, it was a mixture of thud and splash.

Eric stopped squirming; his body went limp. Rob wondered what happened next. Could Eric die a second time? Or would he be a ghost without a head?

As soon as the thought left Rob's mind, Eric's body began to sink into the mud. The bloody pulp of his head sunk in between the grass and mud, leaving a pool of red grass. His body started to sink, like quicksand sucking him down. But Rob knew it wasn't quicksand. It was his remains making the trip to hell.

Rob kicked the victim from his leg and pushed away, sprinting at 8 with all of his strength left.

He collided with the man like a car t-boning a parked car. 8 flew as Rob's momentum knocked both of them to the ground.

Rob pulled out his phone from his pocket with his only good arm, he tried to turn it on, but the rain proved that to be a difficult task.

The man stood up and reached for Rob, Rob tossed the phone into the hole and turned to the man. 8

reached out for Rob, just as Rob landed a well-placed kick to the man's kneecap, buckling it with little effort. Even in death, the man felt his leg collapse and fold in the opposite direction as intended.

Rob took the opportunity to army crawl to the hole, falling in face first. He hit the earth, which was covered in a couple inches of water. Rob started to panic that the phone would be damaged in the water, before remembering that the past version of himself purchased a new waterproof phone.

He struggled until he found the phone, stuck into the mud. He picked it up and cleaned it off with the shirt under his sweatshirt. It wasn't dry, but it wasn't soaked. Rob fumbled around in the mud and water until he pulled out the pistol. Stuck in the mud at the grip and barrel. Rob cleaned out the barrel as well as he could, it seemed as dry as he could hope for.

"God, please still work."

SPLASH!

SPLASH!

SPLASH!

One by one shadows dropped into the hole with him, they reached for him and grabbed at his body. He could make out their faces, all of them had head wounds or at the very least, bloodied faces. They climbed through the water in the crowded hole and began to pull at him. Rob kicked and squirmed, but it was little use. The hole wasn't big enough for him to fight them off on his back.

The phone began to illuminate.

Rob managed to break a leg free, which he used to swiftly kick the closest victim in the chest, sending him flying back into another body.

He slid the green button on the screen.

"Hello?!" He tried to not sound panicked, doubting it went through.

"Um, hi?" Becca said from the opposite side.

"Hey, thanks for helping me," Rob said as he tried (and failed) to fight off the remaining figure.

"Yeah, I hope it helps?" She chuckled. "So, should I start?"

Rob tried to push away the figure with his free arm, which buckled under the pressure of his dislocated shoulder.

His eyes were wide as he tried to not scream in pain, he bit down on his lip and answered Becca: "No, please, wait exactly 30 seconds and go ahead. Word for word."

"Okay," Becca said from the other side. He could hear her unfold the piece of paper from the envelope he gave her. The paper had his phone number and instructions. To call him at 3:15 a.m. and say a couple sentences he had written down for her. He claimed in the note it was a poem that his ex-fiancée, Tess, had written for them. He wanted to hear it again. Rob knew that it would sound weird, he knew that the entire thing was weird, but he knew that a couple hundred-dollar bills slipped in the envelope would ease her a little.

"Thank you, thank you for everything," Rob said as he pressed the mute button on his phone. He wasn't positive if she would hold her end of the bargain if she heard what he hoped would happen.

Rob slammed the phone into the mud above his head, bottom first so the speaker was exposed. The phone stuck from the wall of the grave like a ninja star in a low-budget movie from his childhood.

Rob grabbed the pistol and raised it to his temple.

His arm pulled back, one of the figures had climbed up and now had his arm in a death grip. Rob grunted and tried to free his arm.

The other figures were climbing towards him now, they were almost to his arm as well.

Rob could feel the time slip away as 30 seconds didn't feel like the right amount of time to have told Becca.

Thud!

Rob looked down to see Anna lunging towards him.

He tried to kick a leg free to push her off, but there was no use. The victims had already made that impossible.

Anna climbed over Rob and grabbed for the figure holding on to his arm with a literal death-grip. She pulled away from its fingers as they snapped and popped like twigs.

"Save Jed!" Anna screamed as she freed his arm completely.

Rob brought the gun to his temple and closed his eyes.

The last thought that entered Rob's mind was how crazy this all was. How he had met David that night so long ago to better his life with Becca, and now he was ending it with her help. That he could have been happy with her. They could have been happy together.

The literal last thing to pass through Rob's mind was a bullet.

As the sound rang out in the grave, Becca's voice began again: "Blood for blood..."

CHAPTER SIXTEEN

The following weekend, only 6 days later, a large group of people dressed in their sharpest clothes and almost all in black gathered in a small group.

They stood only a couple feet from where Rob had pulled the trigger days before.

Lanai held Jed's hand as she brought a soggy tissue to her eyes with her free hand.

The ceremony was short, not a single person could fight back the occasional flow of tears. The event was highlighted by random gasps of people trying to catch their breath.

It was hard to understand, no one wanted to talk too much about it. Rob seemed to be full of life. He loved his job. He loved his life. He loved his family.

How could he leave them? Sure, Lanai and him had a rough patch, but that seemed to have worked itself out with a little counseling and time. No one thought of Rob as a man on the edge, someone that needed an ear to talk into. It shocked everyone that ever knew him.

As the evening winded down, the remaining family and friends stayed late at their house to throw back some beers and talk about their favorite stories of Rob. The evening differed from earlier in the day. They cried, but with joy behind each tear. They laughed and smiled enough that occasionally someone would cry out: "Oh my god, my cheeks hurt!"

Jed carried a bottle of his father's favorite beer and sat alone on the back porch. A small fire had been lit earlier, but now it was just small orange embers and smoke.

Jed finished the beer and tossed it into the dying fire, it hissed as the little remains of alcohol spilled onto the burning wood and ash.

"You wanna talk about it?" A voice said from behind Jed.

Jed didn't turn around, "Nothing to talk about."

"Of course there is. Your father, my best friend, just passed away," David sat down beside the young adult.

"He didn't pass away, Dave," Jed said, "he left us."

"That's not fair," David said. "You don't know the full story."

"Do you?" He asked with tear-filled eyes.

David shook his head and took a swig of his own beer, "No, but I'm sure he had his reasons."

The two of them sat there for a while, listening to the fire crack and pop. The night sky was brighter than it had been in years, the moon glowed with authority over the night sky.

David leaned over to Jed and nudged his beer bottle against him, "Drink. Get drunk. Then... come find me."

Jed smiled, "Sure."

"I'm serious."

Jed's smile dimmed, "Alright?"

David and Jed both stood up, David leaned in again, "I need to ask you a question. It might seem strange, and believe me, it will be..."

Jed hesitated; he had never seen David act so out of character. “Yeah, what’s up?”

“What would you do to see your father again?”

ACKNOWLEDGMENTS

I had a handful of people that were integral to finishing this novel. Brianna, I appreciate that you would stay up late with me most nights and brainstorm ideas back and forth for what felt like hours. Some of my favorite stuff in the novel came from those nights. I needed to give a shout out to Patrick Delaney for all the support and positive conversations we had through our publishing process, literally kept my head above water on more than one occasion (IG @patrickrdelaney). I'd also like to thank a few people that stepped up and read the beta versions of the novel and helped me tune it before the release: Ty Huard, Sarizona, Iona Caldwell (https://ionacaldwell.weebly.com/), Patricia Galvan (IG @dreamsofwriting_author), and Amanda Michewicz (IG @skyyness12). And finally, thank you Rob and Dave for letting me borrow your name.

FOLLOW MIKE SALT:
INSTAGRAM: @MIKE_SALT
FACEBOOK: @MIKESALTMOOSE
TWITTER: @MIKESALTMOOSE
AMAZON: amazon.com/author/mikesalt

ABOUT THE AUTHOR

Mike Salt was born in Texas in 1987. His family relocated to Klamath Falls, Oregon when he was 3 years old. In his early 20s he began working for several comic book publishers as either a writer or an art director. In 2013, he began working on his short stories, submitting them to various magazines and collections. Mike Salt joined the USAF in 2014 and is now back in his hometown. He won the Inkshares 2018 Horror Competition with his debut Novel BLIND scheduled for released in 2020. In 2019, he hopes to finally marry Brianna. They have two daughters, Kyla and Lennox, and one son, Justin. The house also has a fluffy dog named Moose and a small fish named Salty.

Made in USA - North Chelmsford, MA
1062680_9781073526109
03.25.2020 1229